ORCANIA

BECAUSE SAVING THE WORLD ONCE IS NEVER ENOUGH

A. E. KEENER

iUniverse, Inc.
New York   Bloomington

iUniverse books may be ordered through booksellers or by contacting:

iUniverse
1663 Liberty Drive
Bloomington, IN 47403
www.iuniverse.com
1-800-Authors (1-800-288-4677)

Because of the dynamic nature of the Internet, any Web addresses or links contained in this book may have changed since publication and may no longer be valid. The views expressed in this work are solely those of the author and do not necessarily reflect the views of the publisher, and the publisher hereby disclaims any responsibility for them.

ISBN: 978-1-4401-7852-8 (sc)
ISBN: 978-1-4401-7853-5 (ebook)

Printed in the United States of America

iUniverse rev. date: 8/9/10

This novel is dedicated in memory of my aunt, Alice Hinson Winburn.
1949–2007

CONTENTS

ACKNOWLEDGEMENTS:

I would like to thank my uncle, Acie Kinlaw, for his assistance with the battle scene between the Toracs and Dirdrom's army. With his knowledge of battle tactics, the battle scenes come to life.

I would also like to thank my editor, Kevin Watson, for proofreading my manuscript.

Finally, I would like to thank my illustrator, Daniel VonSeggan, who, with my guidance, designed the cover.

Trust. A word that is precious to every living individual. It is the foundation on which bonds of friendship are born and peace thrives. Without trust, a human's corrupt desires are free to wreak havoc on the world. These corrupt desires entice the population to succumb to mass killings and pointless suicides for greed and lust. Without trust, the only thing that flourishes… is war.

PREFACE

Darkness settled over the world as one by one the stars awoke. Down below, the wild grass fields sparkled under the light of the moon. The fields were known by the locals as the Whispering Fields. Late at night, if it was really quiet, one could hear whispers rustling through the grass. On this night in particular, they were extremely talkative.

"*There is supposed to be rain tonight.*"

"*I hope my leaves do not wilt.*"

"*The way the weather has been lately, I am afraid I will never take root!*"

"*Someone's coming!*"

"*This way?*"

"*Yes, and that someone is being followed by two others.*"

"*They are running very fast.*"

"*I do believe that the first someone is being chased by the other someones.*"

They immediately lowered their voices and mumbled excitedly over the news.

After a few minutes, a figure appeared running quickly towards the Whispering Fields. Sensing they were about to be trampled, the grasses pulled out their roots and stepped aside to allow the figure to run pass.

The figure was a young woman with emerald green eyes and long red hair that flew behind her as she ran. Flowers were interwoven in her hair. She wore a sleeveless, green silky dress that reached her knees. The bottom of the dress was ripped in several places. A belt made of ivy vines circled her waist. She wore an ankle bracelet made of the same ivy vines. Her bare feet pounded against the earth as her breath came out in short spurts. Fear etched her face as she hurried through the Whispering Fields.

I have got to run. It is the only chance I have left. She could hear her two pursuers a few feet behind her. For the past hour, they had been chasing her relentlessly. The girl sighed, afraid she wouldn't last much longer.

A forest slowly came into view causing the girl to quicken her pace. *It looks like the tide is turning in my favor.* Sensing the change in the girl's demeanor, the two pursuers sped up. The girl accelerated. *This is my last chance. I have got to make it.*

When she was only a few feet from the forest, the girl called out to the trees with her mind.

"Please, my friends, help me."

As she ran into the forest, the trees came to life. The roots pulled themselves out of the ground and swung at the two pursuers as branches tried to ensnare them from above. The girl smiled when she heard her pursuers scream as they were beaten by the surrounding greenery.

The girl continued to run until she could not hear the cries of her pursuers. Knowing she was safe for the moment, the girl bent over to catch her breath. *All I have to do now is get to a temple, and this horrible nightmare will be over.* The girl took several more deep breaths to calm herself and then she stood up.

"My, have we been a trouble maker today," a deep cold voice said from behind her. The color drained from the girl's face. Without looking back, she sent vines hurling toward her stalker as she sprinted off into the forest.

"Brutus, Milo," the voice yelled.

A creature shot out of the shrubbery and pinned her to the ground. The girl struggled against the creature, but its grip was too strong. She tried to call to the trees again, but something blocked her connection. Resigned, the girl glared at her captor. She tried to appear brave, but the girl couldn't suppress the shudder that ran down her spine. Her captor's body was shaped like a lion's, except the two back legs had bird's feet. Scales covered its snake-like head. Its beak made a clacking sound as it opened and shut its mouth. A forked tongue flicked out occasionally as if to taste the air.

The girl, however, was drawn to its eyes. The eyes were snake-like and blood red. They were narrowed and focused on her. The creature looked her up and down as it smacked its lips. It leaned forward and opened its mouth. A deep rattle escaped its throat, and she smelled the scent of rotten carcasses. The creature stopped though when its partner yipped.

The girl tore her gaze from her captor and looked at its partner. The other creature was now wagging its snake-like tail as it waited for its master to come and praise them for their success. The rattling its tail made caused the girl to feel more tense.

A figure stepped out of the shrubbery and walked toward her. It stayed out of any direct light making it seem more like a shadow than a person. She smirked. *It is just like him to hide in the darkness and allow others to do his dirty work.* The creature who had been waiting rushed to its master's side. The figure scratched the creature's head.

"I don't know why you keep running away from me. I am only trying to do what's best for you… for everyone."

The girl's face flushed with anger. "You and I both know that is a lie. You are nothing but a deranged psychopath. I would never *ever* help you." She spat at his feet. The two creatures hissed at her.

The figure sighed as he pulled something from his pocket. "My dear, dear Glade. You act as if you actually have a choice in the matter." He held the object up to the pale moonlight. The girl realized that it was a hypodermic syringe. The figure squirted some of the liquid out of the vial and turned to the girl. She struggled against her captor's grip with renewed determination. The creature pressed down harder on her chest, nearly crushing her lungs. The figure grabbed her right arm and leaned toward her ear. "Oh, and feel free to scream all you want to. There is no one here to save you."

The next morning, the people in the nearby village awoke and began their daily chores. As they went about their day, none of them could shake the feeling that something was wrong. It was then that they realized that the Whispering Fields weren't whispering anymore.

Chapter 1:

A STRANGE BIRTHDAY PRESENT

"WAR has always prevailed throughout the course of history," Mr. Bentbottom droned from his place in front of the blackboard. He was a middle-aged man with balding gray hair and hazel eyes. He positioned his big horn-rimmed glasses so that they sat on the crook at the end of his nose. It made him feel superior to those who were around him. He wore his traditional plaid shirt over brown slacks and a red tie with a picture of an angry Garfield in the center. He adjusted his black belt so that his potbelly did not hang out as much. When the sophomore class first met Mr. Bentbottom, they had the impression from his clashing attire and monotone voice that his class would be as boring, as the phrase goes, as watching paint dry. Unfortunately, their first impression was right.

Today, to everyone's dismay, Mr. Bentbottom's lesson was on their least favorite subject: wars. Before he continued, Mr. Bentbottom scanned the room to see if anyone had fallen asleep or wasn't paying attention. His eyes landed on a girl in the second row farthest to the left. She was petite with bright blue eyes. She wore her golden-blond hair in a ponytail with whispies framing her face. Today, she was wearing a sleeveless red shirt with a pleated jean skirt. Doodling on a piece of paper, she seemed Too preoccupied to hear what Mr. Bentbottom was saying.

"Trixie," Mr. Bentbottom said. Startled, Trixie looked up and smiled at him innocently. Mr. Bentbottom still couldn't believe that this girl, who never paid attention to a word he said during his lessons, had one of the highest grades in the class. He shook his head to clear his thoughts and continued with his lesson.

"Besides World War I and World War II, can you name a war that occured during the course of history?" Mr. Bentbottom asked.

"The War of Roses which was fought between the Yorks and the Lancasters," Trixie said.

"And do you know who took control after the war?" Mr. Bentbottom asked, a smirk appearing on his face.

Still smiling sweetly, Trixie said, "Henry Tutor became King of England after the war."

"Correct." Resigned, Mr. Bentbottom turned back to the blackboard.

As soon as he wasn't looking, Trixie rolled her eyes. *Why does he always pick on me? It's not like I'm the only one who is bored out of her wits.* She felt a buzz in her lap and grinned as she flipped open her cell phone. On the screen was a text message.

Looks like U out smarted Mr. Shiny again!! =)

Trixie grinned as she looked to the other side of the room at Kate, one of her two best friends. Kate was a few inches taller, about five-foot-seven, and sixteen years old. She had bright green eyes and long, beautiful red hair which was usually down. Today she was wearing a pink scoop-neck shirt and a black miniskirt. Kate was now grinning back at Trixie, her phone held under her desk. Trixie looked back at her cell phone and typed a message back.

Mr. Shiny?

Both of them had been trying to pick a good nickname they could call Mr. Bentbottom so, if either one of their phones was confiscated, he wouldn't know that they were making fun of him. Within a few seconds, Trixie received a text message back.

Haven't u seen his forehead in the daylight? The glare from it nearly blinds u!!

Trixie suppressed a laugh. She quickly glanced up to see what Mr. Bentbottom was doing. He was busy pulling out maps of Grecian army battle movements. Feeling she was still safe, Trixie wrote back to Kate.

Short, to the point, and funny. Me like. =)

A few seconds later, Kate wrote back.

So, what were U daydreaming about?

Nothing.

Was it dream boy again?

>=(
So it was dream boy...
No comment.

Trixie and Kate quickly put their phones away as Mr. Bentbottom did another quick survey of the room. He was like a vulture searching for dead and decaying flesh to pounce on. Once he was satisfied, he turned back to his blackboard and continued his lecture. Trixie looked down at her doodle in front of her and sighed. When she returned home the summer of last year, her friends had begged her to tell them about her summer. Of course, she couldn't talk about her journey in Quarteze. They would believe she was crazy and needed to be put in an asylum. Instead, she told a revised tale that her uncle and she devised. The story was that her uncle and she worked in a village on the other side of Mist Island where Trixie met a boy named Leo and his amazing pet wolf, Starla. Her friends were upset that she didn't have any pictures of Leo since they wanted to decide if he was a total hottie or a geek. Trixie refused to tell them what he looked like. She didn't want them to judge him for fear that it would destroy the image of him she had in her head; therefore, Kate decided to call him Dream Boy.

"He is Dream Boy since we have to imagine what he looks like," Kate had proclaimed. Her friends eventually forgave her when she showed them the songfish scale and the music box necklaces. Trixie absentmindedly touched the necklaces that were under her shirt. Everyone always asked her why she wore those two necklaces every day. Always, Trixie tried to find ways to evade the true answer. The real reason she wore the necklaces was because they were one of the few connections to her adventures on Mist Island. They were her only souvenirs of the fight with the Shadow One. Of course, there was the book that she found at the Dark Bastion; but it had remained blank ever since she returned to Earth. The necklaces, on the other hand, still felt as if they had magic in them. Plus, the sentimental value and memories they brought made it hard for her to let them go.

Trixie snapped out of her daydreams and found that she had been doodling again. Her doodling, which before was only lines, now resembled a boy and a wolf. Trixie sighed again as she gazed at the doodling.

There was no denying it. She truly missed both Starla and Leo. She envisioned them in her mind's eye.

"*It has been a year since the incident,*" Trixie thought to the hallucinations. "*As soon as the portal vanished, Uncle Alfred and I went back to my house to spend the rest of the summer with my family. Uncle Alfred had a lot of catching up to do since he hadn't seen us for thirteen years.*" Trixie sighed. "*Our family bonding lasted for three weeks. Then one day, Uncle Alfred abruptly left. In a letter that he left for me, he said he was planning to research portals and ancient civilizations. He had noticed that there were many identical traits the Quarteze society shared with some of our ancient cultures. He believed that societies such as the Greeks and the Egyptians could have known how to open portals to other worlds thus causing cultural diffusion.*" Trixie paused for a second in her mind's speech as she thought of the best way to sum up what she was about to say. "*As for me, I am still getting used to a world without magic and being just another ordinary person in a population around 3.2 billion.*" In her mind's eye, Starla and Leo were sympathetic.

"I wish I could see you again," Trixie whispered.

"Miss Trixie."

She snapped out of her daydream. "Yes, Mr. Bentbottom?" She asked quickly regaining her composure.

Mr. Bentbottom was looking at her with one eyebrow raised. Skepticism was clearly written on his face. He cleared his throat. "Can you tell me what year that the Trojan War supposedly took place?"

Trixie smiled.

It seemed like ages until the final bell rang signaling the beginning of the weekend. Kate and Trixie quickly picked up their books and exited the classroom leaving an awestruck Mr. Bentbottom.

"I've never seen Mr. Bentbottom so dumbfounded in my life," Kate said as soon as they were out of Mr. Bentbottom's earshot. "How do you do it?"

Trixie shrugged her shoulders. "I'm not sure. Historical facts just stick in my mind I guess." Secretly, Trixie believed it was because she had magic. While she was in Quarteze, Trixie had to endure "The Trials," a series of dangerous tests, in order to awaken her magic and receive *The Book of Serenity*, the guide to light magic. Although she was unable to use magic on Earth, she could still feel it pulsing through her veins. If she closed her eyes, she could actually see the connection she shared with it. Starla had once mentioned that users of magic tended to remember more information simply because they were required to memorize intensive and complicated spells. Although she was on Earth, it seemed that the same rules applied.

"*Bonjour mes amies.*" A voice disrupted Trixie's daydreams. Kate rolled her eyes while Trixie turned and waved at the speaker.

"Hey, Wendy," Trixie said as a girl with brown hair and brown eyes ran up to greet them. Wendy was Trixie's other best friend. Today, her hair was up in a French twist; and she wore mini Eiffel Tower earrings. She adjusted her green jewel-cut shirt which she wore with dark-blue flared jeans. Her black stiletto heels clicked as she approached them. Trixie never could understand why Wendy would wear casual clothes with fancy heels. Whatever Wendy's reasoning was, it always caused her to receive the attention from many guys.

"*C'est parfait pour un fête aujourd'hui, n'est pas?*" Wendy asked. Trixie only knew three words in French: hello, goodbye, and toilet, so naturally she had no idea what Wendy was talking about.

"Speak in English, Wendy. We can't understand a word you are saying" Kate said. This time it was Wendy's turn to roll her eyes.

"I said it is perfect for a party today, right?" Wendy wrapped an arm around Trixie's shoulder. Catching on, Kate also wrapped her arm around Trixie's shoulder.

"Yeah, I believe somebody will be turning sixteen today and will be getting her license as well."

"That is *if* I pass my driving test," Trixie said with a blush.

"Don't worry, you'll get it," Kate patted her on the back.

"*Oui, tu conduis très bien,*" Wendy added. Trixie and Kate raised their eyebrows. "I said, yes, you drive very well," Wendy said with a sigh. Trixie grinned. Even if she didn't get her license today, nothing was going to spoil her sixteenth birthday. Ever since she was young, she had believed that sixteen was a special year. Maybe it was because she could drive a car or maybe because her father had always referred to it as sweet sixteen. Whatever the reason, she just felt deep in her gut that something marvelous would happen when she turned sixteen that night.

"So, what time is the party tonight?" Kate asked breaking Trixie's daydream.

"At 7:00. Will you get out of practice in time?" Trixie asked.

Kate was on the school's track team and was one of the best sprinters in the division.

"Yeah, I think Coach will let me off early since I have been on my best behavior." Kate grinned.

They laughed as they headed for the door.

Mrs. Rose, a forty-year-old woman with curly brown hair and hazel eyes, sighed as she put the final touches on the cake she had baked. Although she was nearly exhausted from all the work, she was pleased with the preparations. Any minute now her sixteen-year-old daughter would be coming home. As if reading her mind, Trixie burst into the room. Even though she was breathing heavily, she wore a huge grin on her face. Thrusting a laminated card into her mother's face, she said, "I actually got my license!"

Her mother grinned and hugged her. "I am so proud of you, sweetie!"

"I have to tell you," Mr. Rose said as he walked into the room, "I was sweating bullets a couple of times." Mr. Rose winked at his wife.

Trixie stuck her tongue out playfully. "You're mean. I wasn't that bad."

"No," Mr. Rose said, "but I'm your dad. It's my job to worry."

Trixie cast her gaze towards a two-layer chocolate cake that sat on the countertop. "Is that cake for me?"

Her mother had her back turned and was busy cleaning the oven. "It is for your party tonight, so don't steal any icing before then."

Trixie hastily withdrew her finger. *Curses, fooled again by the mother sense,* she thought.

Her mother continued as if she hadn't paused. "Your friends will be here in thirty minutes, so you might want to get ready."

Trixie nodded, then hurried up the steps to her room.

The first thing Trixie saw when she entered her room was the massive pile of plush toys on her queen-sized bed. Her mother had begged her probably a million times to get rid of some of her toys, but she just couldn't part with any of them. Each toy held a memory of her childhood, although she probably needed to do something about them before they took over her entire room. Trixie shoved the thought to the back of her mind as she walked over to her closet. She decided on a v-neck tank top and a cute black mini skirt.

After dressing and styling her hair, Trixie still had time to spare. Instead of going downstairs to stare wistfully at the cake, she sat down at her desk. Her desk faced a window allowing her to gaze out whenever homework became overbearing. On her desk was the feather of the Twilight Falcon, the strange book from the Dark Bastion, the notepad with details from her trip on Mist Island, and her bamboo plant. Trixie frowned. Over the past few days, her plant had been wilting. Just like the Twilight Falcon had suggested, she tried talking to it and feeding it extra water. It would work; but, by the next day, it was wilting again. Trixie fed it some water and started talking to it. By the time she was finished, the plant's leaves were not drooping and had only a slight brown tinge.

Trixie sighed. There was something definitely wrong.

The doorbell rang. Quickly, she pushed her worries aside as she raced downstairs.

The party was a huge success. They ate pizza and watched movies. Even Tori, Trixie's nine-year-old sister, was behaving. After they finished eating the cake, it was time to open presents. She happily tore into each one of them, egged on by her family and friends. She was on her last present when the phone rang. Her father quickly left the room to answer it. He came back a few seconds later holding the cordless phone in his hand.

"Trixie, it's for you," he said as he held out the phone. His expression was a mix between being slightly confused and amused.

Trixie glanced at her watch. *It's almost eleven. Who would call me at this hour?*

Still bewildered, she took the phone from her father. "Hello?"

"Hello Trixie, it's been a while since the last time we talked." The voice was unusually cheerful, deep, and male.

Trixie nearly stumbled from disbelief. "Uncle Alfred, is that really you?"

"The one and only." Alfred laughed. His laugh sounded forced.

"Is everything alright?" Trixie asked.

Alfred laughed again. "Of course, of course, why wouldn't it be?"

Trixie wasn't sure why; but, the more he talked, the more her worry grew.

Alfred cleared his throat. "Actually, I was calling to let you know that I will be in town tomorrow morning; and I was wondering if we could meet."

Trixie thought for a moment. Both her friends were busy with other obligations, and she was almost sure her parents would go antique shopping.

Trixie shrugged. "Sure, I can meet you."

"Excellent!" Alfred said, his tone back to being overly cheerful. "Meet me at the train station at 8:00 sharp. Oh, and Trixie, Happy Birthday."

Before Trixie could say anything, he hung up.

After saying goodnight to her friends, Trixie trudged back up to her room. Even though she was tired from the day's events, her head was buzzing with questions. *Again, Uncle Alfred has left me with a million questions but not a single answer,* she thought as she opened the door to her room. She glanced at her bamboo plant and frowned. It had only been a few hours, and the plant was already wilting again. She was about to collapse on her bed when she noticed something lying on it. It was a small green-colored book. Silver leaves and vines wrapped themselves around the cover and spine. The symbol of the sun eclipsed by the crescent moon was on the spine and the front cover. It took her a second before she realized that it was the book from the Dark Bastion.

"That's strange. I don't remember putting it on my bed." She reached out to grab it. Before she could touch it, the book flipped open to a blank page.

"It must be the wind," Trixie said to reassure herself that she wasn't hallucinating. She quickly scanned her room. As far as she could tell, all her windows were shut tight. Trixie frowned as she looked down at the book again. She had to suppress a scream at the sight before her. Six words were slowly materializing on the page.

And so the journey begins again…

Chapter 2:

THE T.D.T.

I T was 8:00 when Trixie stepped out of her parents' black Ford Sedan. After waving goodbye, she walked to a nearby bench and sat down. Knowing her uncle, he would probably be late or not show up at all. Trixie sighed as she took in her surroundings.

There were only a handful of people at the station. Trixie guessed they were using the train to arrive at work early. Seeing nothing promising, she focused her attention on the contents in her backpack. Inside were crackers, water, a book she was required to read for school, and the vine-covered book. Hesitantly, Trixie opened the vine-covered book and examined it. To her relief, the pages were blank. Trixie shrugged and put the book back into her backpack. She had been expecting this since she had checked it fifty times before with the same result. She was beginning to think that she had imagined the entire incident. Trixie pushed the thought from her mind as she pulled out her other book and began to read.

It was an hour later and her uncle still hadn't shown up. *Where is he?* Trixie thought as she gazed at her watch for the twelfth time. Trixie felt something cool travel down her face. Wiping it off, she realized it was water. She looked up and groaned. Huge ominous black clouds covered the sky as pearl-shaped raindrops plummeted to the world below.

"Oh, great..." Trixie grabbed her backpack and headed quickly for shelter before the imminent downpour. She reached the space beneath the awning just before the downpour started. Shivering slightly, Trixie leaned against a pillar and gazed out before her. As she watched the hunched over people in gray raincoats and umbrellas hurrying along, something caught her attention. Sitting on a bench on the other side of the track was a young girl. She wore a gray hooded cloak over a pink dress. The hood covered her facial features. Two strands of golden blond hair stuck out from under her hood. What was strange about the girl was instead of trying to hide from the rain like everyone else, she seemed to be enjoying it. Her legs, which were a few inches off the ground, were swinging back and forth as she hummed to herself. Her hooded face was thrown back so that the raindrops could splash on her.

She's going to catch a cold, Trixie thought as she continued to watch the girl in fascination. After a few moments, the girl stopped swinging her legs and humming and turned her hooded gaze towards Trixie. As soon as Trixie felt the little girl's gaze, a prickling sensation ran up and down her body. She felt as if she was experiencing déjà vu. *But this is impossible. How could I be having déjà vu if I haven't even met the girl… have I?* Trixie was about to walk towards the girl when the next train arrived blocking the little girl from view.

The sound of screeching breaks filled the air as the train came to a halt. The whistle whined one last time as steam bellowed out the sides of the train. The car's doors swooshed open. Trixie was surprised when nobody exited the car. Looking around, she noticed that no one intended to enter the car in front of her. As she scanned the station, she heard a slight cough come from the car. Looking back, Trixie's lips curled up into a smile. Standing in the threshold licking his paw was Gyro.

Gyro was the faithful companion of Alfred. His gray, robotic flesh shone in the dim lighting and his ruby- red eyes held a hint of mischief as he cocked his head at her. "Hello Trixie, long time no see."

"It has been a while. How are you?" Trixie asked.

"Fine, fine," He looked from side to side. "My master couldn't come so he sent me. Uh, would you step inside the car?"

"Is everything okay?" Trixie frowned.

"Everything's fine" Gyro said. "It's just that I'm in a hurry."

"Um, okay," Trixie said as she stepped inside the car. The doors immediately swooshed shut behind her catching her by surprise.

Tan seats lined both sides of the car. Every few feet, poles ran from the ceiling to the multi-colored carpet. She and Gyro were the only passengers in the car.

"Is no one else coming?" Trixie asked with a slight laugh.

"No, my master rented it just for us," Gyro said, his tail swishing slightly.

Trixie's eyes widened. "Whoa, when did my uncle become so rich?"

"Um… I think I'll let my master explain that later." He jumped into a nearby chair. The train lurched forward causing Trixie to trip. After she regained her balance, she sat down in the chair across from Gyro and looked out her window.

The rain had turned into a misty drizzle allowing travelers to venture outside their shelters. The little girl with the hooded cape was standing right in front of her bench. She was staring at the train as it slowly left the station. Trixie could almost feel the girl's eyes boring into her. A young man in a tan overcoat with a briefcase walked in front of the girl blocking her from Trixie's view for a second. When he moved, much to Trixie's surprise, the little girl was gone.

"Weird," Trixie said quietly as she tore her gaze from the window and slouched back into her seat.

"What is?" Gyro asked. He had just appeared next to her and was staring at her intently as his tail swished back and forth.

Trixie was a little uncomfortable with the intensity behind his question. She shifted in her seat, "Nothing. It was nothing." She looked out the window and watched the scenery rush by as the train picked up speed. *Still, I would have liked to know who she was.*

"The next stop is Cheyenne Station," Gyro said, bringing her back from her dream world. "We will get off there and take a taxi to where my master is."

"So why isn't my uncle picking us up?" Trixie asked with a slight smile.

Gyro shifted from one paw to the other, "Uh… well… you see… I think my master will give you a better explanation than I can." Before Trixie could comment, he added, "I think you should get some rest. Today is going to be a long day." He quickly curled up in a ball and closed his eyes thus ending the conversation.

∞

The train ride lasted for only 15 minutes. Once they stepped off the train, a taxi cab was waiting for them. Without a word, the driver ushered them into his cab and pulled out of the station.

"So where exactly are we going?" Trixie asked a couple minutes later.

"We're going to meet my master where he is conducting his research," Gyro said as he examined his claws.

"Oh, so like a laboratory?"

"No, a manor actually. Westside Manor to be exact."

Trixie raised her eyebrows in surprise. "Wow, a real manor. It's not every day a girl gets to see a manor."

"Don't get too excited; it's not in the best of shape." He curled up in a ball.

After ten minutes of driving, the cab left the urban area. Green rolling hills greeted Trixie as she looked out the window. Five minutes later, the cab turned down an old dirt road surrounded by trees. Trixie gripped the sides of her seat to prevent herself from being jostled. Poor Gyro clawed his seat desperately as he was tossed from side to side. Finally the cab reached paved road as the manor loomed ahead. The architecture of the grand Victorian style home was truly magnificent. The rose bushes that grew around the manor complimented its reddish-brown color. When they pulled in front of the manor, Trixie noticed the two stone gargoyles grimly standing guard on each side of the entrance. They hardly fit the Victorian style; but, still, they were an impressive touch.

As soon as they were out of the cab, the driver stepped on the accelerator and sped away. Trixie coughed as she tried to wave the newly disturbed dust away from her face. "I wonder why he's in such a rush?"

Gyro shrugged as he walked towards the double doors. "With the way he was driving, he better get out of here fast if he doesn't want me to call the cops."

"Gyro," Trixie said with a frown.

"Don't worry," Gyro said. "I was just kidding. We've already paid him so he didn't have to wait for the fare. He was probably trying to get away from here as fast as possible since this place is supposedly haunted."

"That's just like Uncle Alfred," Trixie laughed. "He's not happy unless he's staying some place that is considered haunted."

Trixie pressed the doorbell. A couple of seconds later, the doors opened revealing Uncle Alfred.

"Hi, Uncle Alfred!" Trixie said as she gave him a hug.

"Hello to you, too. It's so good to see you." Alfred ushered them inside. Much to her surprise, no lights were on; and the furniture was covered with sheets. Alfred muttered to himself as he fumbled around for a match.

"So, are you trying to scare people off by making the manor look as if it were haunted?" Trixie asked with a slight grin.

"Oh no, I just haven't had the time to spruce up the place. Plus, there was no need to unpack since I won't be staying here long. Ah!" Alfred struck a match and lit the candle he was holding. "Much better. Now, how about we go somewhere we can talk. I have a feeling you have a couple of questions for my sudden call."

"Yeah, I do have a few," Trixie said as Gyro and she followed Alfred down the hallway. They took a flight of steps at the end of the hallway. As they descended the steps, Trixie noticed the change in setting and atmosphere. The basement was lit by overhead lights, and high tech machinery outlined the room. In the center of the back wall was a large transparent tube. Off to one side were a sofa, a leather chair, and a table in between.

"Just make yourself at home," Alfred said as he opened a mini fridge. The sofa was cluttered with papers. Trixie quickly gathered them up and set them to the side. She glanced briefly at the paper on top. It was entitled *The Manhattan Project* with a huge coffee cup stain in the center of it. Gyro jumped up on the sofa beside her.

"My master really needs to become organized." He mashed the sofa pillow with his paws a couple of times before settling down.

"Here you go," Alfred said as he handed Trixie a bottled water.

"Thanks." Trixie took a sip of the water.

"My master finds the water but has now misplaced the milk. This world can be so cruel," Gyro muttered.

"Gyro, do you want me to install that manners chip in you?" Alfred asked with a frown.

"No," Gyro grumbled.

Giggling, Trixie said. "This is an amazing lab you've set up."

Alfred fondly looked around the room. "Why thank you. It took a long time, but I think it will be worth it in the end." He glanced back to Trixie. "There I go getting ahead of myself again. To fully understand everything that is going on, I'll need to start from the beginning."

"I'm all ears," Trixie said as she leaned back into the sofa.

"Good." Alfred's expression became serious. "As you know, for the past year I have been searching for evidence that cultural diffusion did happen between Earth and Quarteze. I traveled across the globe to Egypt and Greece and then to the Mayan and Aztec ruins. The similarities between the ancient civilizations of Earth and those of Quarteze were astounding. Now that I indeed had proof, my next step was to find out how it happened. My hypothesis was that a portal similar to the one that appeared on Mist Island existed in those times allowing both worlds to interact with one another." Alfred paused to take a sip of water. "After that moment, the idea of portals appearing fascinated me. Where do they come from? How are they created? What is their purpose? As Starla mentioned once, portals between dimensions exist only when something is imbalanced. But I wondered why should they only exist when there is an imbalance? Was it possible to create a man-made portal? Thus my research began once again."

"Since people don't believe in portals, wasn't it hard to find research?" Trixie asked.

Alfred nodded. "Yeah, I had to go by my hunches rather than scientific reasoning. After a couple of months with no success, I was about to give up. One day, I happened to run into an old friend of mine named Samuel Williams. He is a war veteran and loves to talk about old wars, his favorite being World War II. We were once again discussing the general strategies used in World War II when my friend boldly declared, 'The allies were able to win the Pacific War against Japan all thanks to the atom bomb.' This sparked an idea in my mind. The field of atomic science is still relatively new and full of mysteries. Was there a possible connection between portals and atomic bombs? After conducting research on Nagasaki, Hiroshima, and The Manhattan Project, I finally found what I had been looking for—a connection."

"Wait, the two are connected?" Trixie asked in amazement. "I'm almost afraid to ask. But how?"

"I noticed that during the explosions foreign gases and radiation were emitted in the atmosphere. These new additions, which weren't there before the explosion, had to come from somewhere, from another world perhaps. In Science 101 you learn that an atom is composed of three parts: the protons, neutrons, and electrons. As I think you will remember, Starla once said that the collision of pozitan and negaritan magics helped create tears and explosions in the universe. Wasn't it possible for a split atom to create a temporary tear between worlds? Thus, I created my hypothesis. When an atom is split, it creates a small tear between the dimensions."

"Wow, that is an amazing hypothesis," Trixie said. "But, if atom bombs create tears within the universe, why haven't scientists detected them?"

Alfred nodded. "A good question indeed. We can't see them because, as Starla said, the universe is constantly mending itself. In order for a man-made portal to be created that will last long enough and big enough for detection, a device would need to be created..."

"Oh no, you didn't..." Trixie's eyes widened.

Beaming, Alfred pointed to a long transparent tubular device. "Behold the first man-made portal device prototype. The T.D.T."

"The T.D.T?" Trixie asked.

"It's an acronym. It stands for Trans-Dimensional Teleporter."

"But in order to create a portal big enough to transport something," Trixie said as she stared at the T.D.T, "the amount of splitting atoms must be..."

"Around two hundred," Alfred said, still smiling. "Give or take of course."

"But is that safe?" Trixie asked.

"What I am about to tell you mustn't leave this room," Alfred leaned forward in his seat. "In order to make the T.D.T., I needed sufficient funding. An organization, which shall remain nameless, provided me with the funds and materials I needed. I made the T.D.T out of the same metal that is used for nuclear plants and a new bonded metal the organization created. It hasn't gone on the market yet because it is still in the experimental stages, but I found that the properties in its structure allow it to contain nuclear energy. With a few of my own reinforcements, I was able to create this behemoth you see before you."

He went over to a computer and began to type quickly. "After a few tests, I was able to get a few brief video feeds from another world." He motioned Trixie over. Pointing to the large screen above them, Alfred said, "Watch the monitor. This was one of my first feeds."

Trixie looked up at the screen. An image of golden-green grasslands appeared before her. The camera rotated upward. The sky had a purple hue; and, to Trixie's astonishment, there were three pale moons in the sky. After a moment, the screen faded into black.

"That was amazing," Trixie said.

Alfred's eyes were sparkling. "I thought so as well. I didn't realize though that when I transported a camera to the other world a lot of the battery power was lost. I doubled the battery supply of the next camera I sent." He typed a couple of keys. "Watch the screen again."

The same grasslands appeared on the monitor. This time, however, something was moving slowly through the tall golden-green blades. A second later, a creature popped out of the grass and approached the camera. The creature was similar to a capybara with pale purple fur. Streamer-like feelers attached to its hip bones flowed towards it face. It eyed the camera curiously before touching it with one of its feelers. When the camera adjusted its lens, the creature dropped the camera and scrambled away. With a few feet of distance in between, the creature eyed the camera suspiciously. After a minute, it walked towards the camera again. Both its feelers wrapped around the camera and lifted it up. Then the screen went black.

"Well, I bet you can figure out what happened next. I made a few more modifications to my video camera and sent it one more time." He met Trixie's gaze. "This one, I think, you will find interesting."

This time, instead of grasslands, the video showed a barren wasteland. Explosions were occurring in all directions. The camera was jarred and slowly lifted upward.

Trixie let out a gasp. "Leo."

A boy with brown hair and green eyes stared into the camera. He was slightly battered and bruised. "Please give this message to Trixie Rose," he said as he quickly glanced behind him. "We are in Orcania and need her help. Everything has gone wrong. Glade was..." He stopped abruptly as he looked to his left. His eyes widened. "Wait. No, Starla." The camera was dropped, and the feed was cut.

"Oh my gosh." Trixie clinched her music box necklace unconsciously.

"When I first saw this, I knew that it wasn't a coincidence," Alfred said as he turned to look at her. "I didn't want to show this to you. The T.D.T is only a prototype, meaning objects can be transported to Orcania but cannot come back. If you saw this, then you would be determined to go. The idea of you going to another world by yourself..." He paused as he looked away. "But, I knew it was foolhardy to hide it. Destiny is not through with you. If I didn't tell you, then you would find out some other way." He sighed. "So, instead of you recklessly finding your way there, I will help you." When he saw her frown, he added, "This is your choice. You should not feel as if you have to if you don't want to. Remember, I can send you to those exact coordinates; but I will not be able to bring you back."

Trixie was silent for a couple of seconds. Finally, she shrugged. "It doesn't look as if I have much of a choice, does it? They need my help, and it would be selfish and cowardly of me if I didn't try."

Alfred's shoulders sagged slightly. "I had a feeling you would say that. I was hoping that you wouldn't, but I knew you would." He stood up. "How about we pack you some supplies?"

"Uncle Alfred," Trixie said. "Thank you."

Alfred broke into a small smile. "You're welcome."

After she put her provisions in her backpack, she followed her uncle back to the T.D.T. Now staring at it, Trixie suddenly felt nervous. It seemed a lot bigger and more foreboding than before. Alfred opened the door to the tube. "Step in here, please."

"Are you sure this thing is safe?" Trixie asked as she stepped into the tube.

"All the bugs should have been worked out," Alfred said.

"Wait, what?"

Alfred closed the door and winked at her.

There was only a slight space between the glass and herself. She wrinkled her nose in annoyance. *I feel as if I am in one of those scientific test tubes,* she thought as she glanced around the tube. *Good thing I'm not claustrophobic because it sure is tight in here.* Looking through the glass, she saw Gyro staring at her. He took his paw and saluted her. Trixie grinned and saluted him back.

"You ready to go?" Alfred asked.

"Roger." Trixie held her thumb up.

"Alright. Establishing coordinates," Alfred muttered as he typed on the keyboard.

"**Coordinates established,**" the computer said. "**Initializing transportation in T-minus ten... nine...**" A crash went off upstairs.

"Massster, they're here!" Gyro hissed.

"Already? They weren't supposed to come until tomorrow." Alfred frowned as he stood up.

"**...eight...seven...**"

"Is everything all right?" Trixie asked.

"It's nothing." Alfred motioned to Gyro. "Come on. We've got to delay them."

"Good luck." Gyro followed Alfred upstairs.

"**...six...five...**"

What's going on? Trixie thought as she craned her neck for a better view of the stairs.

"**...four...three**" There was another crash as an alarm went off. The transporter slowly came to life as it began to buzz and glow. "**...two... one...**"

"**Malfunction! Malfunction! Data Error!**" The computer screeched. "**Recalibrating coordinates.**"

She was blinded by a white light.

Chapter 3:

A STRANGER IN A STRANGE LAND

Hᴇʀ skull felt as if it had been cracked in two. *What hit me?* Trixie thought as she rubbed her head and groaned. Slowly, everything came back to her. The strange call, her uncle's explanation, the T.D.T. malfunctioning… Trixie's eyes snapped open as she sat up. As she had feared, she was not where she was supposed to be. Instead of landing in the middle of a barren wasteland, she was in a sparkling bluish green meadow. The sky was a purple hue. Although the sun was out, she could discern three pale moons. "Well, at least I know I'm in the right world, just not in the right place." She looked around in dismay. When she arrived in Orcania, all of the contents in her backpack had scattered. She slowly began to salvage her belongings. The book with the silver leaves was the last item she found. It was sprawled open on the grass. As she bent down to pick it up, a word appeared on the page.

"*Hello!*"

"What the heck!" Trixie dropped the book and crawled back a couple of steps.

"*Well, that hurt,*" the book wrote.

"Uh, sorry," Trixie leaned forward hesitantly. "How are you doing that?"

"*I am an enchanted object from the Dark Bastion, remember? It is my job to act enchanted. I am so glad this world has magic. It took every ounce of strength for me to write in your world.*"

"Oh." Trixie scooped the book into her arms. "So, uh, what should I call you?"

"*You can call me livre, hon, libro …*"

Trixie stared at the book in confusion.

The book expanded and contracted itself as air blew through its pages. *"Just call me Book."*

After an hour of walking, nothing seemed familar.

Book flipped opened in her arms. *"We're lost, aren't we?"*

"No, I just don't know where we are at the moment."

"A.k.a. we're lost."

Trixie sighed as she sat down next to a tree. "Okay, so maybe we're a little lost. You don't have a map in there by any chance."

"I'm a book not an atlas. I only carry information, not pictures."

"So do you have any information about this place?" Trixie asked as she pulled out a snack.

"At the moment, no."

"Well, you are a bunch of help," Trixie said as she tore off a piece of her snack. A loud splash from a couple meters away caught her attention. "What was that?"

"A splash," Book wrote.

"Har-de har har," Trixie said as she strapped on her backpack and scooped up Book. "Let's check it out."

After climbing through some shrubbery, Trixie arrived at a small lake. The water was a pristine blue, which sparkled under the light of the sun. "Wow, it's beautiful," Trixie whispered.

"It sure is. I wonder what's swimming around in it."

Trixie squinted. It was hard to tell from where she was standing, but it looked as if the two creatures who were swimming within the waters were long and rectangular.

"Hmm, I need to get a better look." With Book still cradled in her arms, she slowly descended the hill. Once she reached the lake, the creatures had already submerged themselves. "Huh, they're gone." She frowned as she peered into the water. Slowly, the head of one of the creatures surfaced. It was a greenish blue alligator. It had a long slender snout with two knobs at the end for its nostrils. As the rest of its body surfaced, Trixie noticed the creature's long powerful tail and the four rib-like bones that wrapped around the outside of its body.

"Oh, lookie," Book wrote, *"it's death."*

"I think it's a gharial," Trixie whispered as she slowly stepped backwards. "I saw them on a show on *Animal Planet*. They only eat fish and crustaceans." The second one surfaced and watched her.

"Well, tell them that," Book wrote.

The gharial-like creatures roared as the spikes on their sides extended outward.

"I suggest you run."

Taking Book's advice, Trixie broke into a sprint with the gharial-like creatures close behind. Unlike the ones she had seen on the *Animal Planet*, these gharials' legs were developed for movement on land.

"Why do these things always happen to me?" Trixie moaned as she tried to speed up. Book would have commented if it weren't pressed tightly against her chest. She glanced back a moment later to see the creatures gaining on her. *What I wouldn't give to have the Harp of Oriantist right about now...*

A loud explosion from behind brought her to a halt. Glancing back, she noticed a newly scorched mark on the ground in front of the creatures. Both creatures blinked, stunned by the explosion. Three men on horse-like creatures stepped in between the gharials and Trixie.

"Men," the man on the center horse shouted. "Scare them off." The two men aimed their guns at the ground in front of the creatures. Both creatures backed a couple of steps and hissed. As the men took aim again, the creatures retracted their spikes and quickly raced away. Trixie breathed a sigh of relief as she loosened her hold on Book.

Now free, Book flipped open and wrote. *"You know you nearly squashed me back there. Anyway, I wonder who these guys are?"*

"I do hope you are okay," said the young man who had given the command. He was slightly older than her with short wavy black hair and bright blue eyes. He looked like a knight in his long blue cape and sword. Trixie closed Book as he hopped off his horse and walked toward her.

"Oh, I'm fine. Just a little frazzled, that's all."

"Yes, it seems that there has been an increase in Glarkeyal attacks lately. We haven't been able to figure out what caused these incidents."

"Well, thanks for the help," Trixie said with a slight grin.

The man gave a bow. "No problem at all." He kissed her hand. "Anything for a lady. My name is Mordrid, by the way." He motioned to his comrades. "Those two over there are known as Roger and Calloway."

Roger, a young man with brown hair and brown eyes, gave a slight nod.

"Hey there," Calloway said with a huge grin. He had curly blond hair and green eyes.

"My name is Trixie," she said.

"What's a young girl doing out and about by herself?" Calloway asked.

"Calloway…" Mordrid frowned.

"Oh, no, it's fine," Trixie said quickly, "I was looking for a friend of mine and got completely lost. His name is Leo. He has brown hair and green eyes…"

All three shook their heads. "Sorry, haven't seen him but someone in the city might of," Mordrid grinned. "How about we take you to the city with us and ask around for this Leo."

"Oh, but I've already been a lot of trouble," Trixie said quickly. "I don't want to cause any more problems."

"Not a problem at all. We've got plenty of time. Don't we Calloway?" Mordrid said with a laugh.

"The more the merrier I always say." Calloway motioned to his horse who pawed the ground. "My horse is still in pretty good shape, so why doesn't the pretty girl ride with me?"

The glare from Mordrid made Calloway snort. "Don't worry, Mordrid. I wouldn't dare steal your damsel."

Feeling a blush rushing to her cheeks, Trixie quickly asked, "What horse breed do you have? I've never seen that type before." All three horses were indeed a mystery to her. Their coats were bluish green and looked as if they were made of water. Their long manes and tails were the same color with hints of silver. Behind each cheekbone were two slits very similar to the gills of a fish. Just above their hooves were small fin-like appendages.

"They're sea horses," Calloway said as he patted his steed affectionately. "And they're the best breed of horses, if you ask me."

"Sea horses originally came from the sea," Mordrid said as he rode up next to them. "Because they were so docile, we domesticated them. They are adaptable for both land and sea travel. Their hooves allow them to move fast and easily like their cousins, while their gills and fins allow them quick maneuverability under water."

"The only weakness they have is they can't go long periods of time on land without rehydrating themselves in some sort of body of water," Calloway added.

"Wow, they are really cool," Trixie said as she stroked the horse.

Calloway mounted his horse and offered his hand to Trixie. "May I help you up?"

Trixie grinned as she allowed herself help with mounting. "Why thank you, kind sir."

"Let's go," Mordrid yelled as he raced off. The others quickly followed.

After an hour of riding, a city appeared before them. Trixie gasped in amazement. Unlike the old architecture of Quarteze, Oracania's city was high tech. Skyscrapers crammed next to each other gleamed against the sky. A large iron wall surrounded the entire city.

Book, who was still in Trixie's arms, pushed itself open and wrote, *"That is Crangor City, the capital of Orcania and home of the reigning body of government. The city is considered a melting pot because people from different backgrounds and beliefs come to live here. The people from the villages jokingly refer to it as the Confused City."*

Trixie raised an eyebrow in surprise.

"What? I actually do know a couple things about Orcania. I am not just a handsome book, you know."

"What are you reading?" Mordrid asked from beside her.

Trixie slammed Book shut, startled at Mordrid's sudden appearance beside her. "Oh, it's just an old family book." She could feel Book trying desperately to open itself out of anger from her remark. *I am not sure how these guys would handle an enchanted book, especially one who is as lively as Book,* Trixie thought as she restrained it. "So, what's the name of this city we're about to enter?" Trixie asked as they approached the entrance.

"It's known as Crangor City," Mordrid said, "the capital of Orcania." Book struggled again against Trixie's hold. "It's also where our governing body discuss political matters."

Calloway craned his head around to look at Trixie. "A.K.A., Mordrid's father, the king, and the High Council."

She looked at Mordrid in surprise. "I didn't know you were a prince."

Mordrid shifted uncomfortably in his saddle. "Well, it's not that big of a deal."

"Mordrid," Roger yelled, "the guard wants to talk to you."

"Coming," Mordrid yelled back as he galloped toward the gate where the guard and Roger were talking.

"Good Lord it's a miracle," Calloway said.

"What is?" Trixie asked.

"I think that's the first time I've ever heard Roger talk." Calloway turned his gaze toward the other three.

Trixie giggled as she released her grip on Book.

Finally free, Book flipped open and wrote. *Told you I was right.*

Trixie resisted the urge to roll her eyes as she closed Book. Leaning forward, she whispered, "You are so immature."

Mordrid signaled them to follow. Once they entered the city, Trixie was surprised to see that a whole different world lived on the streets below the skyscrapers. Market stalls bearing all sorts of goods cluttered the sidewalks. Stretching along on each side of the street were four-foot wide canals.

"It's for the water taxis," Calloway said when he noticed her gaze. "The elderly and the handicapped have trouble walking down these streets. Our miniature dolphins tote them to where they want to go."

"Well, that's very nice," Trixie said.

"Yeah, there's only one problem with it…" He was interrupted as a two-foot long gray dolphin zoomed by pulling a device similar to a scooter with a round floating base. Two kids were holding on to the handles as they whooped and hollered. A cop yelled as he chased them down the street. Grinning awkwardly, Calloway continued, "The kids like to take joy rides."

Mordrid slowed his horse as he came next to Calloway and Trixie. "Whoever is in charge of water taxi security is an idiot."

As they passed through the center of the city, Trixie noticed a statue standing against the wall. It was composed of three maidens in gowns. The one on the right was staring at her arms that reached out to the right. Her arms were slightly rounded and her fingers were outstretched. The center maiden's arms stretched upward as if she were trying to grasp the sun. Her face, too, was staring in the direction of her arms. The final maiden's arms stretched out to the left. She was in a similar position as the maiden on the far right. Her face, as well, was looking in the direction of her arms.

"Who are they?" Trixie asked.

"That is the statue of the Three Graces." Calloway pointed to each one. "The far right is Charity, the far left is Compassion, and the center maiden is Hope. They've been here since Crangor City was built."

"They really are beautiful," Trixie mumbled as they passed the statues.

After fifteen minutes of riding through the streets, they reached the building of the High Council. Unlike the skyscrapers, the building was square and made of red brick. *It's not very impressive*, she thought as her companions and she dismounted. After the three men removed the tack and handed them to the stable boys, they nudged their horses toward the lake. The horses neighed with delight as they ran and dove into the water. Seconds later, they resurfaced and zoomed around the lake. Mordrid handed a parchment to Calloway. "Can you two make sure this gets to my father? I want to take Trixie inside, show her around, and help her find her friend."

"Right away." Calloway grinned as he dragged Roger after him.

"You really are too kind, Mordrid," Trixie said.

He gave a slight bow. "Not at all. It is a gentleman's duty to help a lady."

Trixie blushed. As he walked toward the building, Book flipped open in her arms.

"It's a gentleman's duty… I don't trust him. He's way too mushy. If I had a stomach, I'd puke."

"First you would need a mouth," Trixie whispered. "Now behave."

"Did you say something?" Mordrid was looking back at her. Trixie tucked Book under her arm. "Oh no, just taking in the appearance of the High Council's building."

Mordrid grimaced. "I know, it's not all that amazing on the outside but wait until you see what's inside. I bet it will leave you breathless."

Trixie grasped Book tightly, refusing to allow it to write any more comments.

"Wow," Trixie gasped. The inside of the High Council's building was a lot different than the outside. The ceiling was painted like the morning sky and the tiled floor was painted like the grasslands.

Mordrid grinned. "The High Council found the outside to be rather drab. Since it is a landmark, they cannot change how it looks on the outside. The inside, however, can be renovated and changed as much as they please." He walked over to a wall that was completely covered with elevator doors. Pressing a button, he motioned for Trixie to follow him.

"Where are we going?" Trixie asked as the door opened.

"You'll see." He bowed. "After you."

"Thank you," Trixie said as she stepped inside.

The elevator was completely different from the ones she was used to on Earth. The back wall was made of the same bronze material as the door. The sides, however, were made of glass allowing Trixie to see the building's foundation.

"Hmm, let's see… I think we'll go here." Mordrid pressed a button. The door closed as the elevator jerked. However, to Trixie's surprise, instead of going up or down, the elevator went backwards.

Seeing Trixie's confused expression, Mordrid said, "The building was designed outward instead of upward; therefore, our elevators are designed to move from side to side instead of up and down."

"Interesting." She watched rooms rush by. After a minute, the elevator came to a stop and the glass doors to her right opened.

"Here's our stop," Mordrid said as he ushered her out. They walked down a long narrow hallway that was lined with doors. Glancing at a couple of nametags on the doors, she realized the doors must lead to the offices of the council. Reading quickly, she knew that Orcania had a council of agriculture, public affairs, and economics.

Although the hallway's dim lighting was adequate, there were a couple of times when Trixie was forced to squint to make sure she didn't run in to anything.

Seeing her squinting, Mordrid said, "My father believes the dim lighting promotes a better and calmer environment for the employees."

"Well, it was very thoughtful of your father," Trixie said as they rounded a corner. A door at the end of the hallway caught her attention. The light bulbs above the door were burnt out, casting an eerie shadow. Creeping through the cracks of the door and wrapping around its entire frame were vines. "What's in there?"

"Oh, just some scientist's plant experiment. We have trouble with it spreading into the hallway." As he said this, two workmen dressed in blue uniforms walked past them toward the door with hedge clippers in each hand. As they reached the door, Trixie and Mordrid turned into the hallway on their right. Although Trixie did not have the Harp of Oriantist to communicate with the plants, she could almost hear and feel the vines' screams of pain. Suppressing a shiver, she quickly followed Mordrid.

After a few more minutes, the hallway ended at a set of mahogany double doors. With a grin, Mordrid turned the brass knobs and pushed.

The doors opened into a grand throne room. The white marbled floor sparkled, and the red velvet carpet stretched from the doors to the beautiful golden throne. In the corner was a long rectangular table. Flags billowed from the holders in the antique stone walls.

"Wow," Trixie gasped.

"Yeah, I know," Mordrid came to stand next to her. "My father uses this room to meet with foreign ambassadors. It gives the impression that the council is powerful and reliable."

"Well, he was right." Trixie said.

"My Lord," said a green-eyed man with red hair pulled back into a ponytail. "There are people here to see you."

"Can you tell them to wait?" Mordrid asked.

The man shook his head. "They were rather insistent. Said they needed to see you immediately." While he was speaking, two people entered the room.

A huge grin spread across Trixie's face. "Leo! Starla!" She ran over and hugged them.

Leo's appearance had changed since she last saw him. He was taller and more muscular. His brown hair was slightly shaggy, and his green eyes shone with delight. Starla still looked the same. The blue wolf had star-shaped pupils in her emerald-colored eyes and wore a dangling star earring in each ear.

"Mera, we are so glad to see you." Starla said, referring to Trixie by the nickname she had given her.

"Yeah, we were worried you wouldn't be able to make it," Leo said. "When we heard that you were here, we rushed over hoping to catch you. You didn't have too much trouble, I hope?"

"Well, I did run into a little trouble with a couple of Glarkeyals who thought I was going to be their lunch. Thanks to Mordrid and his friends though, I'm all right."

There was a strange expression on Mordrid's face, but it quickly passed as he said with a forced smile, "It was no trouble at all."

Trixie felt Leo stiffen beside her. "Well, thank you for taking care of my friend."

The tension in the room seemed to increase a couple of degrees. Clearing her throat, she said, "I think we'd better go. Thank you so much for your help, Mordrid, and please give Calloway and Roger my thanks as well."

This time a real smile appeared on Mordrid's face as he walked over to her. "I will tell them, and I'm glad that I could be of service." He kissed her hand. "I hope you will come visit again." Blushing slightly, Trixie said she would. When Mordrid released her hand, she quickly gripped Book to prevent it from commenting.

Clearing his throat rather loudly, Leo said it was time to go. Saying goodbye once more, she quickly ran after Starla and Leo.

Chapter 4:

THE TORACS

"So what exactly has been happening?" Trixie asked as they exited the council's building. "Better yet, how were you able to get here?"

Leo sighed. "Well, it was about two months ago when it happened. There were rumors in Quarteze that someone was after Glade, the spirit of the plants. Starla and I decided we would check to see if the rumors were true. So, we went to Glade's temple to speak to her."

"Only to find out we were already too late," Starla's ear flicked. "Someone had indeed kidnapped her and taken her away from Quarteze."

"But, how did you know that her kidnapper took her out of Quarteze?" Trixie asked.

"All the plants were wilting and dying. If Glade were still on Quarteze, the plants would show her distress but not die," Starla said.

Trixie remembered how her plant in her room kept wilting. Could that have been caused by Glade's disappearance as well?

"Also," Leo said bringing Trixie back to the present, "there was the portal we found in a forest nearby. Unlike the one that brought you into Quarteze, this one looked as if someone had taken a knife and sliced through the scenery."

"Therefore, it had to be a man-made portal. The escape route the kidnapper used to escape with Glade," Starla added.

"Whoever kidnapped her must be very powerful if he can recreate a portal," Trixie said.

Starla nodded. "That is what we are afraid of."

"We decided to follow the kidnapper through the portal and ended up in Orcania," Leo said.

They were now back on the streets of Crangor City. Trixie noticed that the poor policeman from before was chasing after another water taxi driven by a couple of kids.

After a few moments, Trixie asked. "Do you have any ideas who kidnapped her?"

Leo and Starla exchanged glances.

"Dirdrom," Starla whispered.

"He was a council member who suddenly rose to power. He's very secretive and is rarely seen in public. Also, his rise to power coincides with Glade's disappearance. A random coincidence? I think not."

Trixie nodded.

"So," Leo began. "That was Mordrid."

"Have you two met before?" Trixie asked.

Leo shook his head. "Nope, but I've heard of him. He seems to be very friendly towards you."

Trixie shrugged. "Yeah, he is a nice guy." She heard Starla snicker. She frowned. "What?"

Leo shot Starla a glare. "It's nothing."

Trixie felt something pushing against her arms. She gasped. "Oh my gosh, I completely forgot. I'm so sorry Book." Leo and Starla exchanged confused expressions as Trixie loosened her hold on Book.

It flew open and angrily wrote, *"I can't believe you forgot about me. I nearly suffocated from your grip. Why wouldn't you let me write anyway?"*

"I wasn't sure they would be able to handle your... tenacity," Trixie said. Looking up, she saw Leo and Starla staring at her in confusion. "Remember the book I found in the Dark Bastion. Well, Leo, Starla, meet Book." She held it up.

"Please to meet you," Book wrote.

"An enchanted book," Leo raised an eyebrow. "I can't believe you still have it."

Starla shrugged casually. "I was wondering when it would wake up."

Trixie and Leo glanced at her in surprise. With a slight laugh, Trixie said, "I almost forgot that you seem to know everything."

"But, of course," Starla puffed out her chest.

As she stared at her two friends, Trixie felt a smile creep across her face.

Leo frowned. "What?"

"It's just, I really missed you guys," Trixie said.

Leo smiled. "We missed you, too."

"Life just is not the same without Mera," Starla added.

Afraid she was going to become mushy, Trixie looked around in an attempt to find a new conversation topic. She noticed that instead of leaving the way that she had entered, they were going in the opposite direction. "So, where exactly are we going?"

Flashing a grin, Leo said, "We're going back to camp. We've been staying with a group of people known as the Toracs."

Trixie raised an eyebrow. "The Toracs?"

"You will like them. They are very nice," Starla said. "Plus, they feed you lots of food." A dreamy look crossed her face. "Mmm, food." The buildings slowly disappeared leaving nothing but desert in front of them.

"We have to cross that?" Trixie said with a frown. The idea of crossing a hot barren terrain was not something she was looking forward to doing.

"Don't worry; we're taking a kadir," Leo said.

"A kadir?" Trixie asked, but Leo was already walking away from her.

Starla motioned to a strange craft up ahead. The base was composed of five logs tied together like a raft. A pole shot out from the center of the raft with a sail attached to it. On the top of the pole was a crow's nest about a foot in diameter. "Orcanians use kadirs to travel across the desert," Starla said, her tongue lolling out of her mouth. "It is a lot easier than walking."

"But how is it powered?" Trixie asked. "There isn't even a breeze." Indeed, the air was dead; and she was already beginning to sweat from the heat of the desert that lay in front of her.

Starla grinned. "We rent a vent, of course." As she said this, Leo walked towards them carrying something white and furry in his arms.

He held the creature up to Trixie. "Allow me to introduce you to our vent, Gnorf."

The creature was a foot in length and resembled a sea otter pup. It had no neck, and its body was two times the size of its head. Fins protruded two inches from its body. Looking up with its big, moist black eyes, it barked, "Gaaaloooo!"

"It's so cute," Trixie said, resisting the urge to reach out and cuddle it.

Book opened itself. "*The Vents are creatures capable of expanding their bodies and producing large gusts when they exhale. Because of their abilities in controlling the wind, they are considered sacred animals to Aktoe, the spirit of the wind.*"

Leo smirked. "Wow, your book sure knows its stuff."

"So, they have spirits here as well," Trixie said.

Starla nodded. "Yes, Orcania's spirits are well known and often visit humans."

"But we can explain all of that later," Leo squinted toward the sun. "It's getting late, and we don't want to be cruising in the desert after dark. The sand sharks could attack us."

"Sand sharks?" Trixie asked as Leo placed Gnorf into its crow's nest.

"Do not worry," Starla said with a grin. "Unless you are small game or get in their way, they are practically harmless."

"I feel *so* much safer," Trixie said sarcastically as she hopped on the kadir with Leo and Starla.

"Take us to the Torac's camp," Leo instructed Gnorf.

Gnorf expanded its body and exhaled. The gust caused the kadir to shoot forward into the desert. After Gnorf maintained a steady breathing rhythm, the kadir coasted easily across the desert.

The ride was smooth, and there were no sightings of sand sharks. In less than an hour, a medium-size campsite appeared before them. As the kadir coasted to a stop, Trixie noted the many tents that cluttered the campsite. "This is the Toracs' camp," Leo said as he tied up the kadir and fed Gnorf. "These guys took us in after we were attacked." Trixie was about to ask about the attack when a man approached them.

"Leo, Starla, I see you have brought company," he said.

Leo nodded as he motioned to Trixie. "Jamul, I want you to meet Trixie."

"Pleased to meet you," Trixie said as she shook his hand. Jamul was tall, dark-skinned and looked to be in his late twenties. He wore a sleeveless white shirt with beige cargo shorts. His whole presence emanated a feeling of friendship and kindness.

"Jamul is the leader of the Toracs," Starla added as she came to stand next to Trixie.

Jamul laughed. "Oh no, I'm not the leader. People just like forcing me to make decisions."

"Don't believe a word he says." A woman approached the group. "If it weren't for him, we would have disbanded a long time ago."

"Trixie, this is Calypso," Leo said. Calypso was a tall woman with long blue hair and greenish blue eyes. Her skin was fair with a bluish tint. Her clothes were made from strange blue leafy material and consisted of a bikini top and a short skirt that tied on the left side. On each shoulder and her lower back were strange tattoos of spiral designs.

"Pleased to meet you," Trixie shook Calypso's hand.

"The same to you," Calypso said.

"Well, how about Calypso and I show you around our little camp," Jamul clasped his hands together.

Trixie smiled. "Sure, I'd love that."

Jamul and Calypso showed her the many different tents and introduced her to the Toracs. Trixie was surprised to see so many different people in one spot. The Toracs seemed to come from every part of Orcania with different backgrounds. There were people from the mountains who were muscular and had squinty eyes. They carefully eyed the group as they sharpened their spears.

"Don't mind them," Jamul whispered. "Mountain people tend to be more suspicious of newcomers. It's understandable since the mountains where they're from sometimes create illusions to confuse them."

A group of gypsy-like people with olive skin and clothes that appeared to have come from the plants hummed and sang as they crushed herbs in clay bowls.

"They are from the forest," Calypso said. "They are very knowledgeable on plant and herbal remedies." There were also groups that looked like Jamul and Calypso.

Glancing over at Calypso, Trixie couldn't help but stare at her tattoos. Calypso noticed and raised an eyebrow.

Blushing, Trixie said, "I'm sorry. I was just wondering how you got those tattoos?"

Calyspo grinned. "Oh, these aren't tattoos; they're birthmarks. Each person from my tribe receives a set of birthmarks at birth." She pointed to the one on her left shoulder. "The spirals represent parts of our personality, our history, and even glimpses in our future." She shrugged. "Though, you need an elder to actually interpret them. No two are ever the same."

Sounds similar to zebras, Trixie thought as they continued onward.

After the tour, Jamul and Calypso left them at their tent and promised to meet them at dinner.

Leo let out a loud sigh as he collapsed on his sleeping bag. "What a day. I'm exhausted."

"You might be," Trixie said as she sat on the ground next to him. "Me though, I'm just confused. When are you going to explain to me about what happened when you sent that message." She paused; then she added as an afterthought. "Better yet, how did you know that I would receive the message?"

"You seem to be forgetting that I am part canine," Starla said proudly. "The camera had your uncle's scent all over it."

"And as for what happened when I sent you the message," Leo propped his head with his arms. "We got caught in the middle of a battle between the Toracs and a group of raiders and their fiends."

Trixie raised her eyebrows in surprise. "There are fiends here?"

"Fiends can appear in any world if they wish," Starla said. "As long as they obey the rules of that world, of course."

"Come again?" Trixie asked.

"Because of each world's physical structure, the laws governing that world are subject to change. For example, in Quarteze it is natural to see unicorns and fiends running about while spirits in their true forms are a rarity. On Earth, magic is never seen; and the laws of science reign supreme. Because of their different physical structures, magic has to adapt." Starla paused for a moment. "These same laws apply to Orcania. Although the spirits are spotted frequently, magic is only used by those that are considered wise or enlightened. Therefore, fiends born in this world have to obey the rules of Orcania."

"So what exactly are you saying?" Trixie asked.

Leo let out a sigh. "Trixie, fiends are created from the hate and greed of people. Since this world does not allow magic to exist by itself, the fiends attach themselves to people who have strong feelings of hate and greed."

Trixie shivered. "That's a little gross."

"That is only the half of it," Starla said. "Because Leo and I used magic, the Toracs believe we are strong warriors sent to help them."

Seeing Trixie's frown, Leo said, "We're in the middle of a war, Trixie."

"What?" Trixie asked.

"It is a fight against the new and old worlds," Starla said. "The new government was supposed to be a godsend to the different villages and cities of Orcania. At first, the structural changes and organization the new government brought helped Orcania; but then..." She glanced at Leo.

"The council claimed that all spirits were outlawed, and citizens were required to shun and ignore them."

"As you can guess," Starla continued, "no one was too happy about that."

"But why would the council do that?" Trixie asked.

"Because, the spirits pose a threat to the new regime that Dirdrom is trying to create," Leo said.

"But you said so yourself that the spirits are close to the people, so why would anyone want to shun them?" Trixie asked.

"The council says that there is no proof of spiritual encounters; and, therefore, they must not exist." Starla stretched her back. "If Dirdrom can make them believe that the spirits do not live among us, then the spirits and people will not be able to band together to stop them. The spirits may rebel against the people causing a war, something that could prove very devastating with Orcania in its current condition."

Trixie's shoulders slumped. "But the High Council can't all be bad." She couldn't believe that people such as Calloway and Mordrid were evil.

"No, it's just Dirdrom who's evil," Leo said. "He's caused all of this upheaval for a rose."

"The War of the Rose," Starla said. "The Sapphire Rose to be exact."

"But what's so special about a rose?" Trixie asked.

Book chose that moment to flip open. "*As the legend goes, the Sapphire Rose is the only one of its kind. It is considered the rose of balance because its petals hold life and its thorns hold death.*"

"It is said whoever possesses this rose can control Orcania," Starla said.

"But no one has ever found it," Leo added. "We believe that is the reason why Dirdrom kidnapped Glade. Because she is a spirit of the plants, she might be able to find the rose." Leo shrugged. "So far though, if she knows, she isn't telling."

"But, why go to Quarteze?" Trixie asked, "Don't they have a spirit of plants here?"

"It is quite possible that Dirdrom is originally from our world," Starla flexed her claws. "If that is true, then he would not have knowledge of the whereabouts of Orcania's plant spirit."

"That doesn't mean he won't try to find it though," Leo added.

"Geez." Trixie exhaled. "So what are we going to do?"

"Try to find the Sapphire Rose before Dirdrom does," Starla said. "That way we can use it to free Glade."

"Sounds like a good plan, so where are we going to start looking for this rose?" Trixie asked.

"Jamul says that the spirits may know where the Sapphire Rose is." Leo pulled a map out and laid it in front of them. "The people of the water know the whereabouts of a water spirit named Aquaritus." He pointed to an ocean bordering the desert. "That's where we'll start."

"Right."

"Oh, I almost forgot." Leo reached for his backpack. "Starla and I have a little surprise for you." He pulled out a beautiful harp that could easily sit in her lap and was made completely of gold. It had intricate swirled designs and runes inscribed on its frame.

"The Harp of Oriantist." Trixie took the harp from Leo. It felt warm and friendly in her arms, as if it were happy to see her as well.

"We were hoping that we might run into you so we brought the harp along. We figured that the Dark Blade and the Harp of Oriantist would be great assets." Starla placed her paw on a long black blade with a red rune painted on its hilt.

"Though, hopefully, we won't have to use them too much." Leo stood up. "Jamul has agreed to be our guide since we do not know our way around here." Helping Trixie up, he said with a grin, "Now, how about we eat some dinner?"

Trixie sighed as she leaned back in her sleeping bag. The dinner had been delicious, and it had been nice to catch up with Starla and Leo. She glanced over at her comrades to find both of them sound asleep... well, Leo, she knew was asleep. Starla, on the other hand, she wasn't so sure about. The wolf had once admitted to her that she did not need sleep but did it to merely pass the time away. Still, she appeared pretty comfortable curled up in a little ball. She glanced over at Book. It lay closed next to her, as if it were pretending to be asleep. Trixie knew better. "You've been quiet."

Book flipped itself opened. *"Je considère la vie et l'orgueille des gens."*

Trixie raised an eyebrow. "You know that I can't understand you."

"Oui, mais ça me rend complêtment impassioné."

Trixie sighed. "Are you writing in French because you are mad at me?"

"Oui."

From listening to Wendy chat in French for the past year, Trixie did know that oui meant yes. "Why are you mad at me?"

"Parce que, tu es un...baka!" Book ruffled its pages in delight.

"Did you just switch from French to Japanese?" Trixie asked, feeling the slight throb in her head worsen.

"Hai."

Trixie let out an exasperated sigh. "Look Book, I can't help you if you won't tell me in *English* what you're mad about."

Book blew air threw its pages. *"It is really sad being a book. People are interested in you one minute; but, when something new and exciting comes along, they throw you aside like you don't even exist."*

Trixie resisted the urge to roll her eyes. She knew that Book was referring to the fact that they had hidden it from the Toracs. After seeing their awestruck reaction to the harp, Trixie was afraid of what they might do to Book...or more importantly, what Book might do to them.

"You know it was for your own safety. You've seen how they react to magical things. They hardly left Starla alone."

Book was motionless for a moment. *"Still, you could talk to me more. I get lonely."*

Like a little toddler, Trixie thought as she smiled. "Well, I'll try. So do you know anything about the Toracs?"

Book puffed itself up. *"Of course, the Toracs are a group of rebels made up of different villages. For example, Calypso comes from the people of the water while Jamul comes from the people of the desert. There are people from the mountains, the plains, and so on and so forth. They have banded together to protect Orcania's traditional of way life from being smothered."*

"Wow, sounds like they're really dedicated if they are coming out here to fight."

"Well, of course. They are trying to protect a way of life from becoming extinct. The spirits and the people of Orcania have benefited from each other over the years. The spirits provide them with the resources to create their food and income while the people create habitats for the spirits to exist in."

"Hey, Book," Trixie said after a minute. "Do you remember when I found you in the Dark Bastion?"

"Yes."

"When you said that your information was needed for another time, did you mean Orcania?"

"Possibly..."

Trixie groaned. "Now you're starting to be as mysterious as Starla." Although Starla was a good friend of Trixie, the wolf had always been mysterious about her past. Whenever Trixie would question her, Starla would always find ways to avoid the answer. She told Trixie that she was an aura, a creature that had the ability to change into different animal forms until it reached its adolescence. Trixie, however, could not believe her.

Book seemed pleased with the comment. *"Well, that is a compliment seeing as Starla is a..."* Book paused as if sensing her excitement. *"She hasn't told you who she is, has she?"*

"No," Trixie said honestly. "But you can tell me."

"No way. I am not putting myself in danger."

"But…"

"Would you two keep your voices down," Starla groaned. She stared at them with one eye open.

"Sorry," Trixie said, suddenly feeling guilty for prying into Starla's past.

Starla winked at her. "Get some sleep, Mera. You are going to need it tomorrow." She closed her eye.

"Good night," Trixie said as she turned over in her sleeping bag. She knew Starla was right. They had a long journey ahead of them. Glancing over at Book, she noticed it had written one more time.

"I think it's best that you still believe she is an aura."

Before Trixie could say anything, Book slammed itself shut.

They were woken up early the next morning to prepare for their journey to see the water spirit. Once Trixie, Starla and Leo had finished packing, they set out to meet Calypso and Jamul on the other side of the camp. When they arrived, they were surprised to see Calypso and Jamul loading their gear on a strange creature. It looked like a cow with a cat's tail. Tied to the tail was a little golden bell. Bangs covered its left eye. Two bones jutted out like boards on each side.

"It's a cowtow," Jamul said. "We use it for transporting goods. The bones jutting out on its sides are perfect to set pottery and ware on."

"Cool," Trixie said as she stroked the cowtow's head. It made a sound similar to a cat's purr. "It's so cute."

"Supposedly, its left eye is magical. The cowtow's bangs cover the eye to protect it." Calypso came to stand next to Trixie. "Of course, no one's sure if it's true because they have never moved its bangs."

"Why haven't they?" Leo asked.

"Because it's taboo." Calypso handed Trixie a pear. "Here, feed it a pear."

Trixie held the pear toward the cow-tow. She nearly jumped when a frog-like tongue shot out of its mouth and grabbed the fruit. It swallowed the pear in one gulp.

"Wow," Trixie said. "That was amazing."

"Yeah," Leo said in agreement.

"It must have a huge esophagus." Starla cocked her head.

Before they could comment, Jamul motioned to them that it was time to go.

Calypso was left in charge of the camp. After leaving Calypso with last minute instructions, they said their goodbyes and left the campsite. Jamul explained that they would be crossing the sands that covered the Underground, a desert city that was buried fifty years before. Supposedly, the city was a technological wonder, housing only the finest and newest technology. Unfortunately, due to its weight, it sunk into the desert, never to resurface again. Luckily, the inhabitants were able to create tunnels out of the city to the surface. They tried to live underground; but, due to the lack of sunlight, most went crazy and returned to the surface.

"We can't use kadirs here because the sand might not support our weight. In some places, the sand is not very stable; and, if you place your full weight down, you may sink into the Underground." Jamul said. "So, stick close."

They were treading cautiously through the sand for over an hour when they heard a loud groan from their left. Glancing over, Trixie saw a large brown shark diving into the sand a mile away from them.

"Was that a sand shark?" she asked.

"Yeah," Jamul frowned. "Though, they don't generally roam around these parts…"

He was interrupted as the ground beneath suddenly exploded. As Trixie was being blown away, she saw a huge sand shark soaring through the air. She felt the ground give way underneath as she was plunged into darkness.

Chapter 5:

THE UNDERGROUND

"**A**RE you all right down there?" Jamul yelled.

Trixie groaned as she sat up and rubbed her head. *What happened?* she thought as she looked around. She saw Leo and Starla slowly getting up. Now she remembered; a sand shark had suddenly surfaced underneath them. When Starla, Leo and she landed, the sand underneath them collapsed, which meant… "We're in the Underground," she whispered.

"Are you all right?" Jamul yelled, sounding a little more panicked this time.

"Yeah, we're fine." Leo glanced up at Jamul with a hand shielding his eyes. "Though the question we should be asking is how are we going to get back up?"

Trixie looked up to see Jamul peering from two stories above them. *It's a wonder that we aren't injured,* she thought.

"Do you have any rope with you?" Starla asked as she came to stand beside Leo and Trixie.

Jamul glanced back to the cowtow. "Yeah, I do, but I don't think it is long enough to reach you." He tried to lower the rope anyway; and, just as he predicted, it was too short.

Trixie, Leo, and Starla cast worried glances at each other.

"How are we going to get out?" Trixie asked.

"There's an exit at the other side of the Underground that leads to a cave at the surface," Jamul yelled.

"Do you think we should try it?" Leo turned his gaze back to Starla and Trixie.

"What other choice do we have?" Trixie gestured around her. "The only other exit is about two stories above us."

"So, it is decided." Starla looked up towards Jamul. "We will meet you at the cave's exit."

"Be careful," Jamul yelled. "The Underground is said to have many traps."

"Great, that's all we need," Leo muttered as they set off down the dark path ahead of them.

"Well, it could have been worse," Starla trotted beside Trixie. "We could have been eaten, or fallen on sharp rocks, or trapped under water, or..."

"Okay, I get the point." Leo glared at Starla. "You two stay close to me. If it gets to the point where we can't see, I can use the sonar spell to help us out."

Trixie nodded as she glanced back at the opening. Although she knew that their only chance for escape was to reach the exit on the other side of the Underground, she hated leaving the opening. She could still see the sky and the outside world. She wasn't claustrophobic, but she wasn't too thrilled over the idea of traveling under miles of sand.

"Come on, Trixie," Leo yelled, startling her from her thoughts. She quickly picked up her pace to catch up with the others.

After walking through a dimly lit tunnel for ten minutes, the trio found themselves standing in awe. The tunnel ended at a long bridge. It was ten feet wide with little foot lights bordering each side. The bridge lead to a beautiful blue-lit city sitting on top of a large rock that attached to the rock wall. Four floodlights were attached to the walls of the cave.

Leo whistled. "Wow, that's crazy."

"Leo, Mera," Starla said, her eyes like huge round plates. "I think we just found the Underground."

"So," Trixie said after a moment, "should we cross the bridge now?"

Starla nodded. "Yes, but remember what Jamul said. The Underground is littered with traps."

They took deep breaths and started toward the bridge.

The walk across the bridge wasn't too bad. The bridge was made of solid rock. The only aspect of the bridge that made Trixie slightly nervous was the gaping darkness beneath them. The floodlights were barely able to penetrate it. *I'd hate to fall down there,* Trixie thought as she suppressed a shiver.

"So far so good," Leo said as they reached the halfway point.

Trixie nodded. "Yeah, we're almost there..." As she said this, she felt a rock give way under her foot. A loud grinding sound echoed through the cavern causing all three of them to pause. After a second, it stopped.

"What do you think just happened?" Leo asked, not daring to move from his spot.

"I do not know," Starla said. She cocked her head as she looked behind them. Leo and Trixie mimicked her actions. A loud crash resonated in the cavern as the bridge started to give way behind them.

Leo's eyes widened. "Run!"

All three raced toward the city.

"Why is there always a collapsing bridge?" Trixie moaned.

"Who cares. I just want to get to solid ground," Leo said.

"Less talking," Starla panted. "More running."

The Underground slowly came closer and closer to the trio as the crashing sound became louder and louder.

It's catching up with us, Trixie thought. She could already feel the rocks slipping away from her feet.

"Almost there," Leo shouted over the sound.

"We're not going to make it." Trixie yelled as she felt the rock beneath her collapse.

"Jump." Starla yelled. All three jumped towards the end of the bridge as it collapsed underneath them. Their feet landed on the edge of the Underground as the crashing sound slowly faded away.

"That was...close." Trixie panted as she doubled over to catch her breath.

"I...hate...booby traps," Leo added as he tried to catch his breath as well.

Starla was lying on her side, her chest rising and falling rapidly. "And to think we have only just arrived in the Underground."

"Don't remind me." Trixie straightened up. After a couple of seconds, Leo and Starla stood up as well. "You guys ready to go?"

Leo nodded. "Yeah, let's go."

The next thirty minutes were spent walking in silence as they studied the many buildings that loomed over them. Trixie noticed that in a couple of places the electricity was still functioning. A sign that said Ray's flashed on and off in time to the faint buzz of the electricity.

"This place gives me the creeps," Leo muttered.

Trixie nodded in agreement. Both Leo and she were startled when Starla stopped abruptly in front of them.

"What's wrong?" Trixie asked.

Starla sniffed the air and let out a low growl. "There is something funny in the air, Mera. I think it would be best if we tread cautiously through this area."

All three took a huge intake of air as they continued walking. As Trixie took a step forward, something whistled past her neck. With a loud thud, an arrow sunk into the building next to her.

"What just happened?" Leo asked as he looked toward the arrow. More loud whistles began to fill the air. Leo's eyes widened. "What the…"

"Run again." Trixie shouted. They could hear arrows whistling behind them and hitting the building as they ran. Trixie was sure that she was going to be hit.

"Up ahead," Starla shouted. Glancing up, Trixie saw two double doors looming before them. Without a second thought, the trio raced through the doors. They quickly closed the doors cutting off their light supply. There were thuds as arrows pierced the wood of the door.

Trixie collapsed to the ground and tried to slow her breathing. *These traps are starting to get very annoying.*

"Hey, Trixie?" Leo's voice drifted from the darkness. "Are you okay?"

"Yeah, I'm fine. What about you?"

"Fine. Starla?"

"I am present and whole, thank you," Starla said cheerfully. There was a slight thumping sound, which meant that she was wagging her tail.

"We need a light." Trixie stood up. "I can't see anything."

"Really?" Starla asked, slightly amused. "I can see perfectly. You should see your expressions. They are very funny."

"Well, I'm glad we are amusing you," Leo grumbled. "Trixie, do you think you can find your harp?"

"I think so..." Trixie began to fumble with the clasp to her backpack.

"It is slightly below your hand," Starla said. Her voice sounded further away than before.

Trixie found the clasp and opened her pack. "Where are you going?" Trixie asked.

"Just get the harp out. I will be back in a moment," she said.

Trixie could hear the clicking of her claws as she walked away. She sighed as she pulled out the harp. "I just hope I still know how to play it." As soon as she touched the harp, her memories rushed back to her. Even in the dark, she found the first string with ease. As she played, a ball of fire began to form in the air.

Starla's face appeared in the dim light. "Here." She held up a piece of wood. "If you light this, then you will not have to use so much of your energy."

"That's a great idea." Leo took the wood and lit it. Starla beamed. As soon as the torch was lit, Trixie put the harp away; and the fireball vanished.

"Shall we continue?" Trixie asked.

"I guess so" Leo held the torch ahead of him. "It looks like this is some sort of tunnel." Both Starla and Trixie glanced down the narrow hallway.

"Well," Trixie said, "following it is probably our best bet."

Starla nodded. "Yes, but we must stick together. Who knows what other traps lie ahead."

Both Trixie and Leo shivered.

After following the twisting turning hallway for over an hour, the trio found themselves stumped. The passageway they had been following branched into three different directions.

"Now what?" Leo asked.

"Do you have any ideas?" Trixie turned to Starla.

She shrugged. "I do not. They all smell the same, so it makes it hard to choose."

Trixie sighed in frustration as she turned her gaze back to the three passageways. She had always hated guessing games. A loud giggle interrupted her thoughts. Trixie jumped slightly. "Hey, did you hear that?"

Starla cocked her head. "Hear what?"

"Someone giggled."

Leo frowned. "I didn't hear anything."

"But I heard someone giggle."

"Mera," Starla said slowly, "I have a canine's sense of hearing, and I did not hear anything other than the sound of our own voices."

"Are you sure you are feeling all right?" Leo asked.

"I'm fine," Trixie said as she crossed her arms and turned away from them. They may not believe her, but she knew what she had heard.

"This way," a voice whispered. Trixie's eyes widened as she glanced to her left. Standing in the passageway was a short hooded figure. It motioned with its index finger for her to follow. When Trixie didn't move, it giggled again before running into the passageway.

"Hey, wait." Trixie raced after it, ignoring the protests of her friends. She wasn't sure why, but she felt that she had to talk to whoever hid behind that hood.

For five minutes, Trixie raced through the dark passageway, flailing her arms out in front of her in an attempt to prevent herself from crashing into a wall. She finally stopped, allowing herself time to catch her breath. The person was gone so there was no point continuing blindly. In less than a minute, Starla and Leo were by her side.

"Why the heck did you run off from us?" Leo asked.

"You had us really worried, Mera." Starla butted her head against Trixie's leg affectionately.

"Sorry I worried you," Trixie said as a pang of guilt ran up her spine. "I thought I saw something; and, well, I just wasn't thinking clearly."

Leo smirked. "I guess we'll forgive you since you made the task of choosing a passageway a whole lot easier."

After fifteen minutes, the passageway ended at a set of doors. After a lot of pushing, the doors finally opened with a loud creak. Light flooded out of the room, forcing them to blink until their eyes adjusted. As they stepped into the room, Trixie let out a gasp. The room was made entirely of gold. Strange hieroglyphics were carved into every inch of the walls, and many different treasures littered the floor. The ceiling was a beautiful replica of the night sky with its different star formations and the eerie three moons.

"This must have been the treasure room," Leo said as he looked around.

Trixie glanced at Starla. She had a strange expression on her face as she sniffed the air. "Hey, Starla?" Trixie asked, "are you all right?"

Starla blinked a couple of times. "Oh, I am fine. I just… never mind." Her gaze drifted to the right. "It seems someone has been living down here."

"What?" Trixie followed her gaze. In the corner was a pile of blankets with chicken bones littering the ground around it.

"But that's impossible," Leo said. "What could possibly live down here for so long…" He was interrupted by a loud growl.

"Well, well, well," said a deep male voice directly behind them, "it looks like I have visitors."

Chapter 6:

ORION

Trixie could not believe what she was seeing. A large black cat with emerald green eyes stood before them. It had a golden clamp on its left ear. Etched into the clamp was the familiar symbol of the crescent moon eclipsing the sun. In the middle of its forehead was a decorative golden eye. It reminded Trixie of an Egyptian eye with elongated sides.

"It looks like a panther," Leo murmured.

The cat laughed, its teeth glinting in the dim light. "I am not a panther. There are no such things as panthers. Although, I can see why you are mistaken. Most people make that mistake. I am technically a black leopard. You cannot see my spots since I have not been in the sun for some time." Grinning, he added, "My name is Orion, by the way. Who are you?"

"I'm Trixie. It's nice to meet you." She continued to eye the leopard warily.

"I'm Leo," Leo added.

Starla just stared at the leopard with one eye twitching.

"Hi, Starla," Orion said with a big grin on his face.

Trixie turned to Starla in surprise. "You know him?"

"Of course," Starla said through clinched teeth. "He is my younger brother."

Trixie and Leo gasped in surprise.

"He's your brother?" Leo asked.

"Yes, I am," Orion said before glaring at Starla. "Although I am not her younger brother. We are both the same age."

Starla rolled her eyes. "We have gone through this many times. I was born before you; therefore, I am older than you."

"Only by a second."

Starla grinned. "That still makes me older."

Orion groaned. "See, this is why I left Quarteze. We always get into fights."

"You ran away." Starla said with a slight growl. "You said that you were going on an adventure of some sort. And did you ever contact me once?"

"Well, you never contacted me."

"I was turned into a statue for Pete's sake. You cannot do much when you are a statue."

"Well," Orion said, "see, even if I contacted you, you would have never known. Therefore, I saved us both a lot of trouble."

As Orion and Starla continued to argue, Trixie and Leo stared in shock.

"So, they're siblings," Leo muttered.

"I guess so," Trixie shrugged. "Who would think Starla's brother was a leopard?" A loud rustling sound came from Trixie's backpack.

As soon as she pulled Book out, it flipped itself opened.

"*So, you were so interested in the leopard, that you forgot about little old me.*"

Trixie blew air through her lips. "Come on Book. We were in a life-threatening situation."

Book bristled its pages. "*Still, I would like to be kept informed.*"

Trixie glanced at Leo who only shrugged. "Hey, don't look at me. There are too many fights going on, and I don't want to be a part of any of them."

At that moment, Orion broke away from Starla and stomped over to Leo. "Well, if Trixie is your mera, then Leo can be my mara."

"What?" Starla shouted. "There is no way you are joining us."

"Hey, Mara." Orion said with a huge grin. "How are you doing?"

Leo shifted uncomfortably. "Fine, I guess."

"Are you even listening to me?" Starla asked, her eye twitching.

Still wearing his grin, Orion glanced back at Starla. "Look, you guys need to find a way out."

"You know how to get out of here?" Trixie asked curiously.

Orion shrugged nonchalantly. "Of course, and I will be willing to show you if you let me come along."

Trixie and Leo looked at Starla uneasily. Starla's face was bright red and her expression looked like she wanted to tear Orion limb by limb.

"*Hm, Starla looks like she is about to blow a fuse,*" Book wrote. "*I wouldn't be surprised if steam started pouring from her ears.*"

"Hey, I am not asking for much," Orion said. "So, what do you say?"

"I say we find the way out on our own," Starla said through clinched teeth.

"*I say, Starla has gone crazy,*" Book wrote.

"Um, can we talk to Starla alone for a quick moment," Trixie asked as Leo and she dragged Starla to a corner.

"Take your time," Orion said as he hopped into his blankets.

Leo leaned toward Starla. "Starla…"

"Please, no," Starla said as she shook her head. "I would rather fight the tarhat again then spend more than an hour with him." She glared in Orion's direction.

"Please, Starla," Trixie said. "We need to get out of here and find Jamul."

Starla stared at the ground as her ears lowered. "Fine."

They all glanced back at Orion who grinned. "Perfect," he said as he headed for the back wall. "Follow me, please." He placed his paw on the wall. A piece of the wall moved away from his paw revealing a passageway. He gave them a toothy grin before entering the passageway. Starla let out a growl but did not voice her thoughts.

They traveled down the tunnel for thirty minutes. Orion was busy talking to Leo as they led Trixie and the still sulking Starla.

"So what's the deal with you two?" Trixie asked.

Starla lifted her head. "What do you mean?"

"You guys don't seem very close."

Starla cocked her head. "You have a sibling, right?"

Trixie nodded. "Yeah, a younger sister."

"Then you know how a sibling relationship is. You love them, but you cannot always stand to be around them."

"So, you two have an intense sibling rivalry going on," Trixie said.

Starla smiled slightly. "I guess you can call it that."

"Hey, sister," Orion called as he craned his neck back. "My ears are tingling. Are you talking about me?"

Starla flattened her ears. "Orion, we have an agreement. Please do not try to jeopardize it."

Orion merely shrugged and continued his conversation with Leo. Trixie let out a sigh as she glanced at Starla. She really hoped Starla would be back to her normal self soon.

After another thirty minutes, the tunnel ended at the mouth of a cave. Standing at its entrance was Jamul and the cowtow.

Jamul looked completely relieved. "Thank goodness you found your way. I was afraid that you would not make it."

Leo and Trixie exchanged sheepish looks. "We had a couple of close shaves," Leo said, "but, all and all, it wasn't too bad."

"After what we went through in Quarteze, we're accustomed to danger," Trixie said with a grin. She glanced at Starla and saw that she had perked up. It seemed the fresh air was helping her.

Jamul eyed Orion curiously. "And who is this?"

Everyone looked at Orion who was busy washing himself.

"It's kind of a long story," Leo said awkwardly.

"Then you will have plenty of time to tell it," Jamul said as he glanced at the setting sun. "It would be unwise to travel the desert at night. At least we know that this cave will be safe from the sand sharks."

Trixie, Leo and Starla exchanged glances. Each was secretly glad they were camping for the night. After the ordeal they experienced, no one was too keen on traveling at the moment.

After finishing their meals, everyone sat by the fire, relaxing after the day's events. Orion lazily licked his paws while Starla pretended to sleep. As Trixie watched Orion, a question popped in her mind. "Orion, how did you get to Orcania?"

Orion grinned. "Oh, it is a wonderful story. You see, about a century ago, I was traveling in Quarteze. I hoped to see new sights and smells. Well, one day, I happened to come across a strange swirling vortex. Unbeknownst to me, that swirling vortex was a portal. I was transported here where I lived in the Underground City."

Starla muttered something under her breath that sounded like an insult.

"So," Leo said, "you've been here for over a century?"

Orion nodded. "The portal closed before I could return, which was one of the reasons I could not contact you." The last part he directed to Starla.

Starla once again was faking sleep.

Trixie sighed. It seemed things were going to be more complicated now that Orion was around.

Chapter 7:

AQUARITUS

THEY awoke early the next morning, planning to do most of their traveling before the afternoon heat set in. After packing their possessions on the cowtow, they began their journey.

"We should have five or six more hours before we reach the end of the desert," Jamul said.

Leo fanned himself as he urged the cowtow along. "Hopefully, we'll make it before the afternoon heat sets in."

"I hope so." Starla panted beside Trixie. "I may be a wolf; but, after awhile, even I have problems with the heat and sand."

"You have problems," Orion grumbled. "Try having black fur. If there is any heat, it is automatically absorbed into your body."

"How are you doing?" Leo asked as he walked beside Trixie.

"Fine," She grinned. "The desert's not so bad in the morning."

Leo nodded as he gazed at the endless orange that surrounded them. "Yeah, it's still hard to believe that I'm here though." He paused as he looked back at her. "And that you are here as well."

The desert was flat and barren. The sand was fine and loose, causing their feet to sink in with each step. When she glanced back, she could barely see her foot prints.

"I know what you mean," Trixie said with a slight laugh. "It's kind of like last time. One minute I'm minding my own business; the next, I'm helping you save the world."

Leo smirked. "Yeah, it seems like we've been doing that a lot as of late."

"I guess saving the world once just wasn't enough."

"Oh dear," Starla said, her expression serious. "It seems my two favorite humans have inflated egos."

"Starla," Trixie glared at her.

Starla playfully pranced around them, her tongue hanging out of her mouth. "Do not tell me you have lost your sense of humor."

After four hours of walking, the heat finally forced them to make camp. Sitting in their makeshift tents, they ate some food as they lazily waited for the heat to dissipate.

"This stinks," Leo flicked a piece of sand off his pants. "Until the heat dies down, we can't do anything."

"I know." Trixie groaned as she swatted a fly. She didn't know how flies could survive in this area, but she was beginning to wish that they didn't. She peered out of their makeshift tent. "I wonder where Jamul went."

"I heard him mention that he was going to check on the cowtow to make sure that it was hydrated," Orion said as he cleaned himself.

"Since Jamul is from the desert, he is better acclimated to this weather than we are," Starla said from her sleeping position.

Trixie nodded as she pulled herself back under the tent. Starla was right, but it still didn't change the fact that they were bored. "I wonder how much farther until we reach the end of the desert?"

Book rustled briefly before opening itself. *"I have a map back here if you would like to see."* It flipped its pages to reveal a detailed map of Orcania

Trixie and Leo looked at Book in disbelief. "You had this all along?" Leo asked.

"And you didn't tell us?" Trixie added. She paused. "Wait, I thought you said you weren't an atlas?"

"I'm not an atlas. Plus, if I told you all my secrets then, I would not be mysterious."

Exasperated, Trixie glanced at the map. Book had indicated with a small dot their position. They were really close to the edge of the desert.

"It looks like we only have a few more hours before we leave the desert," Trixie said as Book closed itself.

"That's good." Leo wiped sweat from his brow as he peered outside the tent. "Let's hope the heat will let up soon."

After an hour, they were finally able to continue. It was near sunset when they finally left the desert and entered the coastal region.

The quick change in scenery surprised Trixie. The sand abruptly changed from orange to white and was firm and compact. A salty breeze drifted through the air as sea oats swayed back and forth from their little mounds.

"We will meet Aquaritus tomorrow," Jamul said as he began to set up camp. "For now, I suggest we get some rest."

It didn't take long for them to set up camp. The damp sand made it easy for the poles to the tent to stay firmly. They had to scavenge around, but they finally found a few dry pieces of driftwood and used them to make a small fire. Off to the right, the cowtow munched happily in its feed bag as its tail swatted the occasional fly.

After she had her sleeping bag laid out, Trixie decided to sit down next to a tree to allow herself some time to unwind.

"You know," Starla said as she walked towards her, "if you listen really hard, you can hear the ocean."

Trixie closed her eyes and listened intently. Indeed, for a brief moment, she heard the faint roar of the surf. She grinned. "I don't know what it is about the sea, but somehow it really relaxes me."

"I agree," Leo said as he and Orion approached them.

"Hey, Starla," Trixie said as she glanced in her direction. "I have a random question."

"What is it?" Starla cocked her head to one side.

"Why is the Harp of Oriantist the weapon for the light?"

"I've been wondering that myself," Leo added.

A smile graced Starla's lips. "That is a good question indeed."

Book flipped itself open and quickly wrote. "*Music is the universal language.*"

"What did it write?" Starla asked.

"Music is the universal language," Trixie said. "It was something that a philosopher named Plato once said."

Starla nodded. "Well, he is right. Music is a language that we all understand. The elements are different in a vast majority of ways. It is hard to communicate to them normally and speaking to more than one at a time is near impossible. Since the harp is a musical instrument, it has the ability to communicate to these different elements through its music."

"You know," Trixie said, "I never thought of it that way, but it actually makes sense."

"Hey," Jamul said as he walked towards them. "Don't stay up too late. We still have to cover a lot of ground tomorrow."

"Don't worry," Leo said, "we were just going to bed."

After saying their goodnights, they quickly went to sleep.

"So this is where Aquaritus lives," Leo said. After packing up their campsite, they traveled a couple of hours until they reached the coast. All that lay before them was a single small wooden pier amidst the vast blue ocean. It was high tide, and the waves were crashing violently against the pier. The force of the waves caused the pier to groan as it rocked and swayed. The wind had picked up slightly, and Trixie could smell the salt in the air. The sand and salt seemed to cling to her skin and clothes making her feel grimy.

"Looks like it," Trixie said. "Is he going to come out of the water to meet us?"

Jamul shook his head. "No, in order to talk with him, you must go into his domain."

Leo's eyes widened. "What?"

"If we go underwater, we'll drown," Trixie added.

Starla shook her head. "Not necessarily. If you create a wind bubble around yourself, then you will not have to worry about drowning."

Trixie let out a sigh as she pulled out her harp. "Okay, I can try. How big should I make it?"

"I'm afraid I'm not going," Jamul said with an uneasy shrug. "I'm a desert person, and I'm afraid my kind aren't too comfortable under water."

"I think I will stay and keep him company." Orion shifted from one paw to another.

Starla smirked. "Still afraid of the water, are we?"

Orion frowned. "No, I just thought it would be nice to keep him company."

"Anyway," Leo quickly cut in, "I guess that means Starla, Trixie and I are the only ones going."

"We better leave our supplies here, just in case we get wet," Starla flicked an ear lazily.

"You'll also need this," Jamul reached into a pouch that was tied at his waist. When he withdrew his hand, he held a smooth, polished blue stone. "Courtesy of Calypso." He handed the stone to Leo. "Since she is from the people of the water, she has a strong connection to the sea. When her people reach adulthood, they receive this stone. These stones come from the deepest parts of the sea so they are very rare and an honor to receive. The stone represents their connection to the water. That way, no matter how far they travel from it, a part of the sea will be with them. Since Aquaratus is a spirit of the water, you should be able to summon him with this."

"Thanks," Leo rolled the stone in his hand. "It feels really light and wet." He handed it to Trixie so that she could examine it. "But my hand's still dry."

"Those stones are mysterious," Jamul said. "Even the elders of the people of the water do not know all of their mysteries."

Trixie handed the stone back to Leo. He pocketed the stone. "But how am I going to use this? I am not one of the people of the water."

"You can use magic," Jamul said, acting as if it was the most obvious answer in the world. "Only sorcerers such as yourself can perform such feats."

"Right, sorcerers," Leo muttered as he threw a glance in Trixie's direction.

"Let's get going," Trixie said, trying to concentrate on the task at hand.

They stood at the edge of the pier.

"Here goes." Trixie took a deep breath as she began to strike the string to summon the air. As the wind began to whip up around them, she envisioned in her mind's eye a circular cocoon surrounding them. As she continued to play the note, she opened her eyes. Just as she had imagined, a circular cocoon of air had formed around them.

"On the count of three we jump in," Leo said. "One."

"Two," Starla said as they prepared to spring.

"Three." Trixie said as they all jumped in.

She felt as if she had entered a whole new world. Colorful purple and pink coral reefs covered almost every inch of the sea floor while fish of many colors swam around peacefully. For a moment, Trixie envisioned herself in a kaleidoscope. The fish reminded her of the swirls and colors she often saw in it. The fish darted quickly, seeming more like blurs of color than animals.

"Now what?" Leo's voice sounded slightly distorted in the air cocoon.

"I suggest you hold the stone out before you and channel your magic through it," Starla said. "Similar to what you do with the Dark Blade."

Leo stared at the stone uneasily for a moment. Taking a deep breath, he held it up before him. The stone began to glow an eerie blue.

"I wonder how long we'll have to wait," Trixie said.

Starla smiled. "Not very long."

A seal popped up in front of them. "Hello dere!"

There was a collective gasp as they stared in shock at the creature before them. The seal was bluish green with strange white designs tattooed all over its body. Its purple eyes stared at them with a hint of curiosity and mischievousness.

Leo was the first to recover. "Are you Aquaritus?"

The seal beamed as he swam around in a circle. "Indeed I am, child." Seeing their surprised faces, Aquaritus laughed. "Oh, were you expecting me to be bigger? Like de whale?" He flipped over. "Dough de whale is amazing, it tends to be too slow. Now de seal is agile and has tons of fun." He swam up close to them with a huge grin on his face. "I like having fun." He playfully swatted at a fish as it swam by.

"We need your help, Aquaritus," Trixie said. "We were wondering if you know anything about the Sapphire Rose."

Aquaritus frowned. "Now, why would you want to know about dat? It's just an old legend. You shouldn't look into it."

"We would not be so interested in it if we were not is such dire peril," Starla said.

Aquaritus cocked his head curiously at Starla. "You aren't from around here, are you?"

"Please," Trixie said. "A friend of ours was kidnapped because of this Sapphire Rose mess."

"Plus, the fighting will only continue until it is found," Leo said.

Aquaritus stared at them, a pensive look evident on his face. After a minute, it seemed he had come to a decision. "De people of da water don't give deir stones freely to strangers unless it is important. I know dat you haven't stolen it because da stone tells me so." He sighed. "Fine, since de people of de water trust you, I will too. De rose does exist, but I don't know its whereabouts. Because of its power, not many spirits know where it lies." He paused. "But, Gardenia, de wood spirit might know. Plants are her expertise. If you were to ask her, den she might be able to tell you." He swam down to the sea bed. "Her forest is a few days north of here." He scooped something off the sea bed and floated towards them. He placed the object on his nose and balanced it for a moment. "Just letting you know dat Gardenia tends to be paranoid." He tossed something into the air cocoon. Leo caught it and held it up so that everyone could see. It was a medium size purple scallop. Aquaritus began to float away. "Show dat to her and she may listen to you."

"Thank you so much," Trixie said.

"I don't dink dat you should be danking me just yet, child." Aquaritus grinned as he flipped. "Dat will only getcha into da forest. Dat don't mean she will meet with ja." He let out a laugh. There was a flash, and then he was gone.

Chapter 8:

THE FOREST OF GARDENIA

Trixie stared at the forest that loomed before her. The trees were packed tightly together and were a beautiful deep shade of green. It looked peaceful, and yet it seemed to have a hint of foreboding as well.

"So," Leo said as he surveyed the scene. "This is where Gardenia lives?"

Jamul nodded. "That's what Aquaritus said."

"So, I guess…we just start searching the forest until we find her," Trixie said.

Jamul shifted his weight uncomfortably.

Starla raised an eyebrow. "Is something the matter?"

Jamul let out a sigh. "The thing is, I'm not one of the people of the forest. Therefore, it would not be wise for me to enter. However, you have magic. Therefore, they will probably be more receptive to you."

"Oh joy," Orion rolled his eyes.

"Fine," Leo said, "we'll go. Just keep an eye on things while we're gone."

Jamul nodded. "Good luck."

Stepping into the forest was like entering another world. The sun hitting against the leaves caused everything to have a green hue. The absolute silence was what unnerved Trixie though. There were no chirping of birds or rustling of forest animals.

"Stay close," Starla whispered, "I do not like the looks of this place."

As they continued to walk, Trixie noticed that groups of leaves were sporadically piled in the forest.

Leo raised his eyebrows. "You think Gardenia is tidying up the place?"

"Hey!" a voice barked from beneath them. "Watch where you're going. I'm sleeping here."

They looked in the direction of the voice. A pile of leaves lay in front of them. One rather large leaf lay on top of the pile. On it was what appeared to be a face.

The face frowned. "What are you looking at?"

"Great," Orion said, "I have been underground for so long that now the leaves talk."

"Er," Trixie said as she tried to regain her composure. "We were looking for Gardenia. Have you seen her?"

The leaf face frowned. "I'm not telling you, and I suggest you leave. You aren't welcome here."

Leo dug his hand into his pocket. "Aquaritus told us to show this to her." He held out the purple scallop.

"Let me see that." As the leaf man spoke, the leaves rose up around him forming a three foot chubby man. Twigs resembled arms, legs, hands and feet. He snatched the scallop from Leo's hands and began to examine it.

Glancing up a couple of times at the quartet, the leaf man finally came to a decision. "Fine, I'll take you to the Baku Tree." He began to walk away. "By the way, the name's Eriol."

They introduced themselves and quickly followed Eriol deeper into the forest.

"So, why are we going to meet the..." Trixie began.

"Baku Tree?" Eriol said. "Because Gardenia is very shy. Heck, I've only seen her once or twice since I've lived here. If anyone knows where she is, the Baku Tree will."

"It seems we have company," Starla eyed the trees.

Trixie noticed figures similar to Eriol watching them from the trees. A jostling from her backpack meant that Book had something to say.

"They're called Macoys. They are spirits who create their bodies from the foliage that surrounds them. When sleeping, they like to take the form of a pile of leaves in order to avoid predators. Lalavines, the spirits who take shape using vines, hide by wrapping themselves around trees."

"Well, would you look at that," Orion said. "Those vines are moving."

Trixie studied a nearby tree. The vines took the shape of a long, leafy plant body as a face emerged to watch them.

"They don't seem too happy to see us," Leo whispered.

"Well, we are technically invading their turf; so I can see why they are cautious," Trixie said.

"If another Macoy makes a snide remark, I swear I am going to bite him," Starla growled.

"Temper, temper, sister," Orion said cheerfully. "You would not want any accidents to happen."

"I would not mind one happening to you," Starla said through clinched teeth.

Eriol cleared his throat, causing them to look up. He had led them into a clearing where a giant tree stood in the center. Its branches seemed to spread out everywhere, and its silver leaves sparkled in the sunlight.

"Oh great Baku Tree," Eriol said as he prostrated himself before it. "I have seekers who wish to speak with Gardenia."

His only response was a loud rumbling sound.

Trixie leaned towards Leo. "Is he snoring?"

"I think so," Leo said.

"He could have a bad case of indigestion," Starla cocked her head.

"Or maybe he can only speak in growls," Orion said. "That would be cool."

As they continued to debate, Eriol peeked up at the tree. "Uh… great Baku Tree?"

At that moment, something jumped out of the Baku Tree's branches. Lowering itself down on a thread was a giant green spider. Vines sprouted from its head, and flowers bloomed on its legs.

"That's an arachlophil, also known as a grass spider. They're very rare and believe deer are a delicacy."

"Joy," Trixie whispered as the arachlophil lowered itself to eye level.

"The Great Baku Tree is currently sleeping. Is what you need extremely urgent?" the arachlophil asked.

Eriol glanced back at the quartet who nodded furiously. "Yeah, Thorn, I'm afraid it is."

Thorn sighed. "Fine." She swung herself into the tree. "Hey, Baku! You have company."

A face appeared on the tree as it began to wake up. "Huh, what? Oh…" He smacked his lips as he looked around bleary-eyed. "What is all the commotion, Thorn? Are we under attack?" His voice sounded old, yet there was a lilt to it.

Thorn swung herself away from him, disappearing into his branches. "You have visitors."

Trixie and Leo jumped as Thorn placed a leg on each of their shoulders.

"Speak up; he's hard of hearing." She quickly swung herself to her original position hanging beside the Baku Tree.

The Baku Tree blinked at them a couple of times as his leaves changed to a ruby red. "Humans in our realm? Why the devil did you allow them in here?"

"Please, we need to speak to Gardenia," Trixie said.

The Baku Tree's leaves changed to an amethyst purple. "You weed to peak to Sardenia?" He glanced at Thorn. "What the devil are they talking about?"

Thorn rolled her eyes. "They said they need to speak to Gardenia."

The tree's leaves returned to a silver color. "Oh, well, why would I tell her whereabouts to a bunch of humans?"

"Show him the scallop," Starla whispered to Leo.

Leo nodded and pulled out the scallop. "Aquaritus told us to show this to Gardenia if we wish to speak to her."

The Baku Tree frowned. "Hmm? What have you got there? Let me see it."

Thorn lowered herself down to take the scallop from Leo before bringing it up to the Baku Tree's eyes.

His leaves changed to a yellow topaz. "Oh! This is Aquaritus' shell. Well, why didn't you say you were friends with him in the first place?"

The quartet resisted the urge to groan.

"It is like talking to a wall," Orion whispered, which caused him to receive a sharp rap on the head from Starla.

Loud snoring filled their ears as they looked up to see that the Baku Tree had fallen asleep once again.

Thorn let out a loud sigh. "Every time..." she swung herself at the Baku Tree once more. "Hey Baku! Wake up already."

"Huh, what? Oh, you're still here?" The Baku Tree stared at them as his leaves returned to a silver color.

"Yes," Trixie said through clenched teeth. "We need to speak with Gardenia. Do you know where she is?"

"What?" The Baku Tree said. "I can't hear you."

"She asked if you know where Gardenia is," Thorn yelled.

The Baku Tree winced. "You don't have to yell." He glanced down at the quartet. "She just left for the Council of Ten meeting in the Shamballa Mountains."

"WHAT?" Trixie and Leo yelled.

"My, everyone is awfully loud today," the Baku Tree said.

Starla sighed. "I guess we will have to meet her there."

"Are you crazy?" Eriol said as he approached them. "The path to the Shamballa Mountains is extremely dangerous."

"Not to mention you would have to avoid the Shinobi tribes that roam around its base," Thorn said as she appeared beside them once more. "They aren't as nice as us."

"We don't have a choice," Trixie said. "It is extremely important that we talk to her as soon as possible."

Thorn shrugged as she returned to her position beside the Baku Tree. Seeing his confused expression, she said, "They're going to the Council of Ten meeting."

"Didn't you tell them it was dangerous?"

Thorn shrugged. "Yes, but whatever it is they wish to discuss with her seems to be too important to wait."

"Well, take the scallop. It may help you," the Baku Tree said. Thorn tossed the scallop at Leo.

He caught it and quickly pocketed it. "Thank you for your help."

"You have an infestation of kelp?" The Baku Tree frowned. "Oh my, I'm afraid I can't help you with that."

"He said thank you for your help," Thorn yelled.

"I can hear just fine. You don't have to yell," the Baku Tree said before turning his attention to the quartet. "You're welcome, and I wish you luck on your journey."

It seemed like forever before they reached the entrance to the forest. Jamul stood waiting for them, a frown evident on his face. A strange white bird sat perched on the cowtow, preening its feathers.

"Something the matter?" Trixie asked as they approached him.

"This." Jamul indicated the letter in his hand. "It seems our base camp was attacked while we were gone. No one was hurt, but they did make a mess."

"I'm glad no one was hurt," Trixie said.

Leo winced. "Aw, man, I'm so sorry."

Jamul shrugged. "When you're opposing something, it tends to happen a lot. The problem is that they need me back there…" He trailed off.

"Go," Starla said.

Trixie nodded. "We understand. They need you."

"Besides," Leo said, "we're going to the Council of Ten meeting in the Shamballa Mountains."

Jamul raised his eyebrows. "You know that place is dangerous."

"Death, destruction, imminent doom," Orion said. "Yeah, we have heard."

"But, we have no choice in the matter," Trixie said.

Jamul sighed as he rubbed the bridge of his nose. "The path that leads to the Shamballa Mountains is not far from here. I'll take you there; but, after that, I'm afraid you're on your own."

"Sounds good," Trixie said as she readjusted her backpack.

"Oh, and you might want to grab some supplies from the cowtow." Jamul rubbed the back of his neck. "I'm afraid cowtows aren't suited for where you're going."

"That's fine," Leo said, "we're used to traveling light. Isn't that right, Trixie?"

She nodded. "Yeah, we'll need a few supplies like food, water, and bedding; and we'll be good."

Jamul looked relieved. "I appreciate your understanding."

After gathering the supplies they needed, they headed towards the path. The journey was silent because no one really knew what to say. Once they reached the path, all eyes turned to Jamul.

"I guess this is where we part ways," Jamul said.

"Good luck," Trixie said with a slight wave.

"The same to you," Jamul waved back. "You are going to need it."

Chapter 9:

THE AMBUSH

THE path was long and twisting, which annoyed the quartet to no end. Much to Trixie's chagrin, the whole atmosphere seemed to be reflecting their mood. The sky was gray and overcast, while the only sounds they heard were the occasional bullfrog.

"This is creepy," Orion said. "I can see why no one likes to travel down this road."

"No kidding." Leo gripped the hilt of his sword. "My nerves are about fried from constantly listening for an ambush."

"Actually, I am enjoying this." Starla pranced around them. "The abundant terrain, the fresh air…"

"The random bullfrogs," Trixie added.

"They are all quite enjoyable."

Leaning towards Leo and Trixie, Orion whispered, "She says that now only because I said I do not like it."

Starla sniffed the air as she looked at the sky. "I think we ought to make camp. It will be dark soon."

"Let's set up here." Leo dropped his backpack on the side of the path.

"Good idea," Trixie said as she placed her backpack to the side as well.

After setting up, they ate their dinner. As they sat contently by the fire, Trixie noticed Orion's eyes were closed. The golden eye in the center of his forehead unnerved Trixie. It seemed almost alive. She jerked when the golden eye blinked and swiveled toward her.

"Ick!" she shrieked.

Starla glared at her brother. "Orion, quit doing that. It is creepy."

Orion opened his eyes and lifted his head. "Oh, and your one eye open thing is not creepy?"

"Can you actually see out of that eye?" Leo asked curiously, hoping to avoid a fight between the siblings.

Orion sighed. "In a way. I only see auras with it."

"Like the creatures in Quarteze?" Leo asked confused.

Starla shook her head. "Those are different, although they were named auras because they shared similar characteristics. Auras in this sense are the energies that radiate from your body."

Orion nodded. "Exactly. You see, your body produces energy that hovers around it. I can see that energy. Auras take the color of your mood. For example, if you are sad, then the color of your aura is blue. If you are angry, then your aura is red. If you are confused, your aura is a mixture of colors and so on and so forth." He wiggled his eyebrows. "The best part about seeing auras is that I can tell when someone is lying."

"But how does the golden eye allow you to see auras?" Trixie asked.

At this point, Book flopped out of Trixie's backpack and opened up.

"*Simple. It taps into the Ajna Chakra.*"

"The Ajna Chakra?" Trixie asked.

"It is also known as the forehead chakra," Orion said as he leaned back on his haunches. "The chakra in your forehead allows you to develop a sixth sense or transcendental awareness. The golden eye channels this chakra's energy so that I can see the auras."

"What he does not tell you is that he was terrified to have it put on his forehead," Starla said with a sly grin.

Orion stuck his tongue out. "Like you are one to talk." He took on a falsetto. "But mommy, I do not want holes in my ears."

"You little pest." Starla immediately ran after Orion who bounced around the campsite gleefully.

"It's still weird to think Starla has a sibling; but, yet, they act just like any siblings would," Trixie said with a slight laugh.

Leo nodded. He glanced over at Trixie. "You know, with everything going on, I never asked you what you have been doing for the past year."

Trixie looked at him in surprise. She was so caught up with finding the Sapphire Rose that she had forgotten that they had never talked about the past year. "How about we catch up now?"

"Sounds good," Leo said with a grin. "So what's been going on with you?"

Trixie shrugged. "Nothing much. School, friends, and I just got my license." Seeing Leo's raised eyebrow, Trixie said, "In order to drive a car in my world, you need to get a license. So, what about you?"

"I pretty much spent my time rebuilding the town," Leo said. "The damage was immense."

"Yikes." Trixie winced. "I'm sorry we couldn't help."

Leo shrugged. "No big deal."

"So," Trixie said hesitantly. "Did you meet any interesting people?"

Leo raised an eyebrow. "What do you mean?"

"You know." Trixie shifted uncomfortably. "Interesting friends?"

Leo's eyes widened in realization, "Oh, no, not yet." He rubbed the back of his neck awkwardly. "What about you?"

Trixie quickly looked away. "No, not me either."

They both jumped when Orion popped up in front of them.

"So, what are you two talking about?"

He was promptly tackled by Starla.

"Feel better?" Trixie asked as Starla trotted toward them.

She nodded. "Yes, Mera, I do."

A rustle to their right caused them to tense. Leo reached for his sword while Trixie's hands rested on the harp. They stood still for a few minutes.

Leo sighed as he put his sword away. "We can't forget that we're in dangerous territory."

Starla nodded. "You are right. We should not let our guard down." She circled three times before laying down. "Now, how about we get some sleep. I believe we will have a long day ahead of us."

They went through the traditional routine of eating and packing before setting off once more. The sky was still overcast, and the only sounds they could hear were their footfalls, which echoed in Trixie's ears as she unconsciously gripped her harp.

Leo shifted his gaze from side to side. "I keep getting this feeling that something is going to happen."

Orion frowned. "Something is not right."

Starla stopped in her tracks as she sniffed the air. "Do you sense it?"

Orion paused to sniff the air. "Yeah, something is coming."

A twig snapped behind them. They quickly whirled around and came face to face with what appeared to be a group of bandits.

They were men who hadn't shaven or cut their hair in weeks. The whites of their eyes were showing, and a chain on each of their arms connected them to strange grotesque canine creatures.

"Are those fiends?" Trixie asked as a man pulled out a knife.

"Yes." Starla eyed them carefully. "Be careful, Mera. They are not like the ones from Quarteze."

With a growl, the man with the knife charged at them. Starla and Trixie scattered as the knife sliced at the exact place they had been standing.

Chaos broke loose. The bandits attacked, swaying back and forth as if they were in a drunken-like stupor. One swiped at Leo's chest. Leo bent backwards to avoid the knife but found himself toppling into another bandit. A fiend snapped at him, but he rolled to the side, pulling out his sword, and swiping at it.

With feral sounds, two bandits charged at Trixie and Starla. Their nails were long and sharp. Trixie had to resist the urge to gag as she sent a plant spell towards them. The plants wrapped around the two bandits, but a second later they both broke free. Orion and Starla dodged attacks while casting uneasy looks at one another.

"This is bad," Leo panted as he stood guard next to Trixie. "I don't want to hurt them."

It wasn't the bandits' fault, but rather the fiends connected to them. The bandits were probably not even aware of what was going on. Starla smacked a bandit with her tail, disarming him. Orion growled as he swiped at a bandit.

As she dodged a bite from a fiend, Trixie glanced around for some sort of cover. Unfortunately, there were no trees or hills to hide behind. All that surrounded them were flat grasslands.

The bandits abruptly stopped their attacks. They stared wide-eyed at the quartet for a moment. With howls, they quickly retreated.

"Okay," Leo said as he hoisted the Dark Blade over his shoulder. "What just happened?"

Orion's and Starla's growling caused Trixie and Leo to look behind them. There was a sharp intake of breath within the group.

Standing before them were a group of people wearing different animal masks. "I recognize them from Jamul's description," Starla whispered. "They are the Shinobis."

Before they could react, nets were thrown over them. Trixie struggled with the net, pulling and pushing in hopes of finding a way out. Instead, the net wrapped around her even tighter so that she could barely move her arms. As she struggled with the net, Trixie found herself looking at a figure wearing a white wolf mask. Tilting the mask up slightly, the figure held a blowpipe to its mouth. A sharp pain shot through her neck as she felt herself spiraling down into oblivion.

Chapter 10:

THE SHINOBI TRIBE

*T*RIXIE *frowned as she rubbed her eyes. No matter how many times she tried, the darkness never abated.* Where am I? *She thought as she slowly stood up. Giggling started up behind her. Whirling around, she found herself in a dimly lit forest. The light casting an eerie blue color and the feeling of déjà vu nearly overwhelmed her.*

"Why are you here?" a young female voice asked.

Trixie stared at a nearby tree and saw a small hooded figure peering from behind it.

"What are you searching for?" the figure asked.

Trixie took a step forward, and the figure took a step backward.

"What are you searching for?" the figure repeated.

Trixie shook her head. "I don't understand. Who are you? Where are we? How did I get here in the first place?"

The figure giggled. "You ask many questions; yet you give no answers." She began to run away.

"Wait," Trixie said as she quickly followed her.

"Follow, follow." the figure said as she looked behind her. The figure turned around and began to run backwards. "What are you searching for?"

"Stop!" Trixie yelled as she tried in vain to reach out to the figure.

"What are you searching for? What are you searching for?" the figure said over and over.

"Stop!"

"Mera!"

Trixie awoke with a start. She found herself looking into the concerned eyes of Starla.

"Sit up slowly," Starla said as she helped Trixie up. "You are still drowsy from the effects of the tranquilizer."

"What happened?" Trixie asked as she rubbed her head.

"You tell me," Starla eyed her carefully. "You kept yelling stop in your sleep."

Trixie flushed as she recalled the dream. "It was nothing. I must have had a reaction to the tranquilizer." Her eyes widened as she remembered what had transpired before she was knocked out. "Are we..."

"Yes." Starla nodded. "We are in the Shinobis' camp. They separated us from Leo and Orion and took the Dark Blade and the Harp of Oriantist. I have already tried the door, but it is barred. It seems we have to wait until we meet with their elders."

"Darn." Trixie spotted her pack and quickly retrieved it. To her relief, Book was still inside.

"*Stupid Shinobis. They threw me aside like I was a piece of trash. As if.*"

"What do you know about the Shinobis?" Trixie asked.

"*Well, the masks our captors wear are not for show. They represent their connection with the spirits and the animals. They always wear their masks outside their homes. Most of the elders know and practice magic. They aren't fond of outsiders, which we've seen.*"

"Our best bet is to convince them that we are not their enemies," Starla said.

A loud knock came from the door. Trixie quickly shoved Book into her pack as the door opened. A muscular man wearing a bear mask stepped inside. He pointed to them and motioned for them to follow. Silently, Starla and Trixie complied.

They were slowly paraded through the camp. It seemed all of the Shinobis came out to watch, some out of curiosity, others out of anger, and even others out of fear. They stopped in front of a large tent. The man motioned to the flap. Trixie gulped as she followed Starla inside.

A table stood before them stretching to each end of the tent. Eight elders—four women and four men— were seated there. Kneeling in front of them were Leo and Orion.

Leo gave a weak smile as Trixie and Starla came to kneel beside him. An elder wearing an eagle's mask cleared his throat. "Our laws state that whoever trespasses into our lands is to be killed."

"However," said the woman elder wearing a doe mask to his right, "because you are traveling with spirits, we have decided to hear your case."

Spirits? Trixie looked at Starla and Orion. *Do they mean Starla and Orion?*

The elders turned and stared at Leo.

Shifting uncomfortably, Leo said, "We came here to speak to Gardenia who is attending the Council of Ten meeting."

Murmuring immediately ensued among the eight.

"If you only wish to speak with her, then why do you carry these?" said a woman wearing an owl mask. She motioned to the Dark Blade and the Harp of Oriantist that were lying on a nearby table.

"They are to protect us from those who would want to hurt us." Starla glanced at one of the guards. "Is that not why you are carrying blowpipes?"

The elders looked slightly miffed by the comment.

"Please." Trixie looked at each of the elders. "We must speak with Gardenia. A spirit, our friend, was kidnapped; and we believe that Gardenia can help us."

"And why do you believe that she will be able to help you?" asked a man in a rhino mask.

Trixie and Leo glanced at each other unsure of how to explain to the Shinobis what they believed.

"Because, we believe that she knows the whereabouts of the Sapphire Rose," Orion said.

A gasp emitted from the elders.

A woman with a swan mask stood up and slammed her fists against the table. "The Sapphire Rose is forbidden. It is the reason why there is a war."

"The war was not caused by the Sapphire Rose but rather by the greed of a few people who wish to use it," Starla said.

"How do we know you aren't like them?" a woman in a crane's mask asked. "Where is your proof?"

"This." Leo held out the purple scallop. "Aquaritus himself gave it to us."

The woman in the crane's mask crossed her arms. "How do we know that you didn't steal it?"

"You don't," Trixie said with a sigh.

The elders looked pleased.

"But," Trixie said causing everyone to look at her, "before you pass judgment on us, please listen to me." She balled her fists against her knees. "A man named Dirdrom is also after the rose. He is dangerous and wishes to take over Orcania by using the power of the rose."

"He stole our friend, Glade, the plant spirit, so that she could locate it," Leo said.

Trixie nodded. "We just want to find our friend and make sure the Sapphire Rose stays in the hands of those who will not abuse it."

The elders were silent for a moment.

"We must discuss the matter," the man in the eagle mask said. "You will stay here until we reach a decision." The elders stood up and left the room.

The quartet sat quietly. They were afraid to speak or move since the Shinobis were watching them closely. Plus, they hadn't failed to notice the gleam of the blowpipes that were strapped to the Shinobis' belts.

After fifteen minutes, the elders returned. They all sat down, excluding the woman wearing the doe mask.

"It's very rare that we actually accept any outsiders' excuses." She gazed at the quartet. "Since you are accompanied by spirits and they do not seem bewitched in any sort of manner, we have decided to grant you passage. You will stay in our camp for the night and must not leave our sight. Tomorrow morning, we will take you to the entrance of the grounds where the Council of Ten meeting is held. Is that clear?"

Trixie grabbed Leo's hand and gave him a smile. He smiled back, his shoulders relaxing slightly.

They were ushered outside to a huge bonfire. The entire village was gathered around it doing animal-like dances. The Shinobis greeted them warmly as they walked by. The news had spread that the newcomers were trustworthy. The quartet sat on a nearby log and watched the festivities.

While the Shinobis danced, they sang and chanted in a beautiful, lilting language. Although Trixie could not understand them, she could tell that each dance represented a story.

A woman in a white wolf mask walked up to them. Trixie recognized her from when they were captured.

"My name is Lita. I am sorry about before." Her voice held a slight accent that sounded like a mixture of Italian and French. "Please take these as an apology." She handed the quartet dark brown drinks before grabbing one for herself.

"Thank you." Trixie sniffed the beverage before taking a sip. A fruit blend overwhelmed her senses. "This is really good."

"We use this drink to keep ourselves connected to the spirits," Lita said as she took a sip. "This drink is made from the fruits of the Oracle tree. The juices from this fruit promote clarity and spiritual awareness."

"Lita," Leo said, "what exactly are the dancers doing?"

Lita grinned. "They are recreating how the spirits work in the world. We do this every year at this time." She cocked her head slightly. "If you don't mind, I would like to ask you a question as well."

"Go ahead," Trixie said.

"We sensed when we caught you that you weren't from this world. Is that true?"

Trixie and Leo traded glances before nodding.

"Trixie comes from a world called Earth while we are from a world called Quarteze," Starla said.

"Why do you ask?" Orion cocked his head to the side.

"We, the Shinobis, do not wish to travel to other worlds; but we are still curious about them." She sighed. "Are your worlds engulfed in war like ours?"

Leo laughed. "We just had a war a year ago."

Trixie nodded. "Yes, my world is experiencing war as well."

Lita's shoulders sagged. "It seems that no world is safe from war. That's nice to know. That means our world isn't defective."

"I think it is our nature to want to fight," Trixie said. "As the saying goes, there is always that one kid who, after seeing you create a building out of blocks, wants to tear it down. But, you know what else I think?"

Lita looked at her curiously.

"I think also it is in our nature to care. Because someone will see that little kid crying over the remains of his building and will come over and help him put it back together."

"Trixie is right," Leo said. "There will always be war; but, if we are willing to trust the people who wish to help clean up the mess, then maybe we are not as doomed as we believe we are."

Lita grined. "You two are very wise for your age."

"That is because they are around us all the time," Starla grinned.

Trixie playfully nudged her head.

"You might want to go to bed soon," Lita stood up. "You've had a long day and still have a half-day's journey ahead of you before you reach the meeting place."

With a slight nod, she left.

The next morning, the quartet quickly packed their belongings and headed out. The Shinobis quietly watched them leave. Their expressions were a mixture of sadness and reverence. The hunters from before accompanied them to the meeting grounds. They surrounded them as they walked, the blowpipes clasped tightly in their hands. By midday, they reached the entrance to the meeting grounds.

A large stone archway stood before them with a stone staircase that seemed to go up forever.

Placing a hand on both Trixie's and Leo's shoulders, Lita said, "this is where we leave you. Good luck with your quest."

They said their goodbyes; and, in a flash, the Shinobis were gone.

Chapter 11:

THE COUNCIL OF TEN

The climb up the stone staircase was long and dull. To pass the time, Trixie decided to pull Book out.

"So," Trixie said, "what can you tell me about the Council of Ten?"

"The Council of Ten is composed of the strongest ten spirits. They hold a meeting every year to discuss matters that are occurring in the world. Their names, if I remember them correctly, are Gardenia, Aquaritus, Plue, Plague, Terra, Aktoe, Electra, Icia, Ore, and Infernia."

"They sound interesting," Trixie said with a slight grin.

"I cannot believe that you are able to walk and read at the same time," Orion's eyes widened. "That takes a lot of skill."

"Or, she is able to concentrate better than you," Starla said.

"Why do you always have to one up me?" Orion asked.

"Because I am older than you," Starla grinned.

Orion scrunched his nose in annoyance. "We are not starting this argument again."

"Uh, guys?" Leo said causing everyone to look up. "Does anyone know how to open the really big doors?"

Two giant stone doors stood before them. Spiral designs were etched on them, and the handles were slightly out of their reach.

"Any ideas?" Trixie asked.

"Try that knocker over there," Starla pointed to the left door.

There was a brass knocker just within arm's reach.

Taking a deep breath, Leo approached the door. He rapped the knocker twice before stepping back and waiting.

A slot at the top of the door slid back to reveal a pair of eyes.

"What do you want?" a voice asked.

"We're here to see Gardenia. We were told that she is here," Trixie said.

Leo pulled the scallop out of his pocket. "Yeah, Aquartis told us to show this to her."

The eyes squinted. "Hmm, so it seems you do have something of Aquaritis'?" The sound of wheels turning came from within as the doors opened.

A brown mouse stepped forward. He wore a Robin Hood-like hat. He crossed his arms and raised an eyebrow at their bewildered expressions. "What?"

"Nothing," Leo said as he shook his head. "Can you take us to Gardenia?"

The mouse huffed. "Yes, though she isn't going to like it."

They followed him inside.

"I'm Bartleby, by the way. I'm the keeper of these grounds, " the mouse said as he led them down a hallway.

As they introduced themselves, Trixie examined the hall. Beautiful paintings lined the walls and vases sat on tables. An elegant red carpet ran down the hallway.

After ten minutes, they came to the end of the hallway. Bartleby held a finger to his lips before opening the door.

Immediately, the sound of voices filled their ears.

"Aquaritus is late," said a giant brownish red bird with a feather sticking out of his forehead. Trixie assumed that he was Aktoe, the spirit of the wind, because she noticed that slight breezes emitted from his body.

"How is this new? He is always late," said a whitish blue polar bear who wore a tiara made of icicles. Ice patches had formed at her feet. Trixie assumed she was Icia.

Bartleby cleared his throat. All eyes turned to them.

"Who do you have there, Bartleby?" Aktoe asked.

"These travelers come to speak to Gardenia." He held up the purple scallop. "Aquaritus seems to believe they are trustworthy."

A golden lioness snorted. "Aquaritus is too willing to trust the humans." *Electra,* Trixie thought as she noticed sparks crackling across her body.

"You shouldn't be so hard on him," said a giant red lizard. *Infernia*, Trixie thought as she noted the small fireballs that would flare up and fade on her body.

"Yeah," said a brown mare. She had a long mane and tail. It was obvious that she was Terra because she smelled of freshly dug earth. "Plue seems to like them."

Glancing over her shoulder, Trixie was surprised to see a purple cat floating beside her. Its bright blue orbs stared at her as it grinned.

"Plue!" He said as he nuzzled his head against her cheek.

"Plue is insightful," said a giant black bear with red eyes and white markings covering his body. Trixie assumed he was Ore since a giant metal hammer leaned against the wall next to him.

A stag with glowing green eyes approached them. A strange greenish mist came from his mouth. "I'm Plague, spirit of sickness." The deer laughed as he saw Leo take a step back. "Don't worry. I'm in the prevention side, not the spreading side." He glanced at Plue. "The guy hovering over your heads is Plue, the spirit of happiness."

Plue grinned. "Plue!"

"He doesn't say much. Most of the time, he is either quiet or singing his total nonsense songs," Plague said with a smirk. He quickly introduced the others, and Trixie was proud to see that she had guessed correctly. "And, finally," Plague said. "There's Garden..."

Everyone frowned as they looked around.

Electra sighed, "I'll go find her." She quickly exited the room.

"You'll have to excuse Gardenia," Plague bent his head and grinned sheepishly. "She's been a tad bit..."

"Paranoid," Ore said with a nod.

Plague shrugged. "Well, that is true."

"Ta-li Ta-lu. Ta-li Ta-lu. Oh, what are we going to do?" Plue sang softly. "Where do we go? Oh, where do we go? To find the lost buffalo."

As she listened, Trixie couldn't help but feel happy. It was something about his singing that made her want to join in.

Infernia squinted her eyes at Starla and Orion. "You are powerful, yet I have never seen you before."

"My brother and I are from another world," Starla said.

"In fact all of us are," Orion added.

Terra raised an eyebrow. "Oh, you must tell us how you got here."

"I don't know. Oh, I don't know. Where to find the lost buffalo," Plue sang. "Ta-li Ta-lu. Ta-li Ta-lu. What am I going to do?"

"I won't go in," a high-pitched voice yelled. "They're going to kidnap and eat me."

"Don't be ridiculous," Electra said as she appeared once more. "They are going to do no such thing." She dragged behind her a very frantic greenish white rabbit. She had a tiara and a necklace made out of ivy. A flower earring accented each ear. She was kicking and screaming as Electra brought her in. Getting annoyed, Electra picked her up by the nape of Gardenia's neck with her mouth. Gardenia ceased in her thrashing and her screaming. Her whiskers still quivered as her gaze darted about the room.

"Please," Leo said cautiously, "we just want to ask you a couple of questions about the Sapphire Rose."

Immediately, Gardenia resumed her thrashing and screaming. "I won't! I won't! I won't! You're just like the others. You're going to steal the rose, kill me, and then eat me."

"We would never do such a thing," Starla said.

Orion shrugged. "I do not know. Rabbits are rather tasty."

Gardenia let out a loud moan.

Starla promptly stepped on his paw as she growled. "You are not helping."

"Please," Trixie said as she held her hands out. "We have a friend, Glade, who is a spirit of plants as well. She was kidnapped by the ones you speak of, and they are trying to force her to tell them where the Sapphire Rose is."

"Are you willing to stand by and allow a fellow plant spirit suffer?" Leo added.

That seemed to hit home because Gardenia stopped her thrashing and screaming. Her whiskers quivered as she stared at them. "They kidnapped a fellow plant spirit?"

Trixie and Leo nodded.

Tension left Gardenia's muscles as her body relaxed. Electra set her down.

Gardenia leaned back on her hind legs as she rubbed her front paws together. "I suppose I could tell you a little bit about the Sapphire Rose..." She said softly.

"We would greatly appreciate it," Leo said as Trixie nodded.

Gardenia sniffed. "The truth of the matter is that I do not know the whereabouts of the Sapphire Rose."

"You don't know?" Trixie asked, her voice raised slightly.

Gardenia winced. "We all used to know where it resided; but, because it is so powerful, we erased its whereabouts from our minds. The one who still has that knowledge is Shal Ron Lee, the spirit of knowledge."

Plague nodded. "Yeah, he knows everything. He lives in his floating library that resides in the three moons' grasslands."

"So, how do we get there?" Trixie asked.

The Spirits stared at them in surprise.

"You intend to find Shal Ron Lee?" Terra asked.

"We really need to find the Sapphire Rose," Starla said. "If we do not find it before Dirdrom, then I am afraid this world is doomed."

"Dirdrom." Aktoe's eyes narrowed. "I've heard of him. He's the reason why we do not live in harmony with the humans anymore."

"Then we must prevent him from achieving his goal," Icia added.

Gardenia sighed. "You will have to travel east for four days to reach the grasslands."

"Two of those days are in the null void zone," Infernia added.

"What is the null void zone?" Orion asked as he cocked his head.

"The null void zone is a place in Orcania where magic cannot work. It is something about the magnetic field surrounding that area that prevents magic from working," Aktoe said.

"But just because there is no magic, that doesn't mean there aren't any creatures that wouldn't love to take a bite out of you," Ore said as he crossed his arms.

"Two days..." Leo said.

"Without magic," Trixie added.

"Leo, Mera, I know you can do it," Starla said.

"Plus, what choice do we have?" Orion added.

Gardenia's ears twitched. "Well, if you are that determined..." She fiddled with something on her neck before placing it in Trixie's hand. Trixie gazed down at a small pink bud. "Hopefully, this will be able to help you."

"Thank you," Trixie said as she pocketed the bud.

"It's the least I can do. You are trying to save one of my kind," Gardenia said with a weak smile. "With it and the purple scallop, Shal Ron Lee will listen to you."

Bartleby cleared his throat behind them. They all glanced back and saw that Aquaritus was standing with him.

Aquaritus raised an eyebrow. "So, what did I miss?"

Chapter 12:

THE NULL VOID ZONE

Aﬀer leaving the Council of Ten's grounds, the quartet found that they were experiencing a mixture of emotions. They were glad to be one step closer to finding the Sapphire Rose, yet they were dreading the journey through the null void zone. None of them knew what to expect, and that was what they feared the most.

"I wonder what lives in the null void zone," Trixie said in an attempt to break the silence.

"Who knows," Leo said with a shrug. "Let's hope that we can handle them."

"When do you think we'll reach the null void?" Trixie asked.

Starla let out a howl.

Trixie and Leo were surprised to see Orion and Starla twisting and howling in agony.

"What's wrong?" Trixie asked.

"Obviously, the null void affects all types of magic," Starla said through clenched teeth. "Including magical creatures such as ourselves."

"What's going to happen to you?" Leo asked.

"We have to return to dormant forms," Orion growled. "It is up to you now."

With a pop, Starla transformed into a small statue while Orion was absorbed into his golden eye. They both fell with a thump.

For a couple of moments, Trixie and Leo stared at the objects in stunned silence.

"We're alone," Trixie said, trying to ignore the fear rising inside of her.

Leo drew his sword and held it in front of him. "Well, there's nothing we can do." He picked up the golden eye and stuffed it in his pocket. Numbly, Trixie nodded as she picked up Starla's statue and cradled it in her arms.

They were alone now. Without any magic. Without any help.

"It's weird lighting a fire the old fashioned way," Trixie said with a slight laugh. After, they had set up camp, Trixie and Leo spent a tedious amount of time trying to light the fire.

"Yeah," Leo threw a stick into the fire. "You never appreciate magic until it's gone."

Trixie brought her knees up to her chest. "Hey, Leo?"

Leo stopped poking the fire to look at her. "Yeah?"

"How are we going to do this without magic?"

Leo shrugged. "We'll just make do with what we have."

Trixie pulled Book out and glanced through its pages. Book was in a dormant stage as well. "That's easy for you to say. You're the one with the sword. What can I do with a harp? Serenade them to death?"

Leo came over and sat down beside her. Placing a hand on her shoulder, he said, "Don't worry. We'll get through this. I promise."

Trixie nodded, feeling somewhat reassured. She wasn't sure why, but hearing Leo's words seemed to make her feel better. "Okay."

"Good," Leo said as he patted her shoulder. "Now, get some sleep. I'll take the first watch."

After a restless night, they began their journey, keen on getting out of the null void zone as soon as possible. Not hearing Starla's and Orion's bickering was beginning to make them anxious.

Their thoughts were interrupted as a loud shriek rang through the air. "What was that?" Trixie asked.

"Don't know." Leo looked around anxiously. "Let's keep moving."

Trixie nodded as she hurried after him. Her shoulders went rigid when she felt something rustle in her backpack. She quickly reached inside and grabbed Book. Opening it up, Trixie was surprised to see it trying to write something.

"I...da...rac..."

"What's wrong?" Leo asked.

"It's Book," Trixie said as she showed it to him. "I think it's trying to tell me something."

"But it shouldn't be able to say anything since we're in the null void zone," Leo said.

"Well, it must be important if it is trying so hard," Trixie said.

"I...da...ra..."

Growls rumbled around them. Trixie looked at Leo, fright evident on her face.

"What was that?" she whispered.

The growls grew louder as a figure emerged from the brush. It had the head of a wolf, the body of a leopard and the tail of a crocodile. Its fur was black, and its eyes were blood red. It bared its teeth as four other figures appeared behind it.

"Back up slowly," Leo whispered. Taking a step toward them, the other creatures bared their teeth as well.

"Leo." Trixie refused to take her eyes off the creatures. "I think we need to run."

Leo nodded. "On the count of three."

"Three," Trixie said as they bolted.

The creatures followed, howling. Logs and vines littered the ground causing Leo and Trixie to trip a couple of times. Trixie tripped on a vine. Her leg banged into a log as she scrambled to her feet. Ignoring the pain that shot up her leg, she hurried after Leo. The creatures moved quickly and were slowly getting closer. If they hadn't been running for their lives, Trixie would have admired how graceful the creatures looked when they ran. They had to come up with a plan and fast.

"Any...ideas... how to...throw...them off?" Trixie asked between breaths.

Leo frantically looked around for inspiration. His eyes widened.

"You see... that river...there?" he panted. "Head for it."

Trixie quickly caught on. If they were in the river, the creatures wouldn't be able to smell their scents.

Taking a deep breath, Trixie forced all her energy into a sprint. They quickly covered the few feet between the river and themselves and dove in. The shock from the cold water made Trixie want to scream. Murky water filled her mouth as she swam quickly to the surface. Reaching the surface, she gasped for air. She coughed as she spit water out of her mouth before diving back in.

The river was moving at a lazy pace, allowing her to swim easily. Leo grabbed her hand and pulled her to the surface. They broke the surface of the water and quickly hid behind a rock. Breathing heavily, they watched the shoreline.

Moments later, the creatures appeared. They sniffed the air as they ran back and forth along the shore. The creatures soon gave up and let out several yelps before they sped off.

"Do you think we're safe?" Trixie asked after several moments had passed.

Leo nodded. "Yeah, for now. Let's just swim downstream for a little bit before going back on land."

By nightfall, they were cold, wet, and exhausted. By chance, they found an abandoned cave.

"At least we have a place to sleep tonight," Leo said as he sat his pack down.

Trixie sneezed. "Yeah."

Leo frowned in concern. "You need to get out of those damp clothes so you won't get sick."

"So do you," Trixie said. She glanced over at a large rock. "I'm going to change over there."

Luckily, their backpacks were waterproof. Trixie quickly stripped and put on a spare set of clothes. She checked on Book and Starla to see if they were in good shape before stepping out from behind the rock.

Leo had changed as well and had already started a fire. He gave a weak grin when she came to sit by him. "So, that was interesting."

"That's one way of saying it." Trixie sighed. "What a day."

They both looked at each other and laughed.

"I don't know why I'm laughing," Trixie said. "What happened wasn't funny."

"I'm going to be so glad when we are out of this place," Leo said as he fished some food out of his backpack.

"I can't wait to use magic again," Trixie said. "Then I wouldn't feel so helpless."

"But you have to admit; we did a pretty good job, under the circumstances," Leo said.

Trixie nodded as a slight smile appeared on her lips. "Yeah, I guess we make a pretty good team."

She was in the forest again. Glancing to the side, she noticed the hooded child sitting on a rock. In her hand was a parchment.

"*Who are you?*" *Trixie asked.* "*And how am I the only one who sees you?*"

"*To dream of a rose is to dream of love. One that has no limits. One that is pure and whole.*" *The hooded figure looked at Trixie.* "*Does that sound familiar?*"

The scenery melted away and was replaced by a bedroom. The room gave the illusion that it was a garden of sapphire roses. Even the furniture had roses carved into them.

"*I remember this place,*" *Trixie said as she looked around.*

"*Everything is connected,*" *the hooded child said from behind her.*

Trixie turned around to face her. "*What do you mean?*"

The hooded child cocked her head. "*Why are you here? What are you searching for?*"

Trixie quickly sat up, placing a hand on her chest.

Leo placed a hand on her shoulder as he frowned. "You okay?"

Trixie nodded. "Yeah, just a weird dream." Once her breathing calmed, she asked, "Hey, Leo? Do you remember the bedroom from the Dark Bastion?"

Leo nodded. "Yeah."

"Do you remember what was in it?"

Leo laughed. "How could I forget? That room was covered in..." his voice trailed off as his eyes widened. "Sapphire roses."

"Do you find it odd that all of a sudden we have to find a Sapphire Rose?"

Leo shrugged. "It could be a coincidence."

"I suppose," Trixie said. She was unsure; however, Starla once said that nothing happens by coincidence. "Everything is connected," she whispered as she lay back down. *I wonder if that really is true.*

The next morning they started out early, hoping to avoid any encounters with the creatures from the day before. They didn't speak because they were putting all of their energy into walking.

By midday, they had almost reached the edge of the null void. Exhausted, they decided to take a quick break to gather their energy.

Trixie took a sip from her canteen. "I don't remember the journeys in Quarteze taking this long."

Leo wiped the sweat from his brow. "Well, we weren't running for our lives with nothing to defend ourselves with."

"Point granted." Trixie put the canteen back in her pack. "You ready?"

A loud growl came from the brush nearby. Immediately, the five creatures from before leapt out and began to circle Trixie and Leo.

Leo quickly pulled the sword from his sheath and held it in front of him. "I don't know if I can handle all of them."

Think, think, think. Trixie looked around. She could feel the creatures sizing her up.

"*Hold out Gardenia's gift and cover your ears.*"

Trixie frowned. *Who said that?*

"*Hold out Gardenia's gift and cover your ears.*" The voice repeated in her mind.

"Leo, cover your ears."

"What?" Leo looked at her as if she were crazy.

"Just trust me."

Frowning, Leo slid the Dark Blade back into its sheath and covered his ears. Immediately, Trixie grabbed a cloth that was dangling from her backpack and stuffed it in her ears before pulling the bud out. As soon as the sunlight hit it, the bud blossomed into a pinkish purple flower and began to sing.

"Lullaby, lulla, lulla, lullaby. La, la, la, la, la, la." The creatures' eyes changed from bloodthirsty to sleepy. As the flower continued to sing, the creatures began to yawn and wobble. After a minute, they fell asleep. Trixie and Leo looked at each other in surprise. As carefully as possible, they stepped past the creatures. From the way they were snoring, Trixie knew they would be out for a while. When they were out of hearing range, Trixie stuffed the bud back in her pack. As soon as it was out of the sunlight, the bud stopped singing.

"Good thinking," Leo said as they began to walk away.

"Thanks."

Loud rustlings emitted from their packs. Without hesitating, they dumped the contents of their packs. There was a pop and Starla and Orion stood before them.

"I feel nauseous," Orion said, wobbling slightly.

"Are we out of the null void?" Starla asked as she looked around with her ears perked.

"I guess so," Leo shrugged.

Trixie hugged Starla. "I'm so glad you are back." Starla chuckled.

Book flipped open. *"I see you survived the racars I tried to warn you about. How did you get past them?"*

"With this," Trixie said as she picked up the bud.

"That's a Lullaby bloom. They sing whenever they absorb sunlight. Their singing can cause anyone within hearing range to fall asleep. It's often used to cure insomnia."

"It's a lucky thing that we have it then," Trixie said with a grin.

As soon as their supplies were packed, they continued on their journey.

Chapter 13:

THE THREE MOONS' GRASSLANDS

THE scenery changed drastically once they left the null void zone. Decaying woods were replaced by rich gold and green grasslands that rustled every time the wind flowed through them. They could see the purple sky once more and the faint outline of the three moons.

When nighttime came, they made camp once more. As they settled down, Trixie stared dreamily at the sky. The three moons seemed closer than before. She could discern the craters on each moon. Stars twinkled lazily in the sky, and she was suddenly overwhelmed with a feeling of serenity.

"What are you thinking about?" Leo asked as he sat down beside her.

"Just how peaceful this place is," Trixie sighed. "I can see how these grasslands got their name."

"Yeah, the moons are really pretty here." Leo leaned back on his hands.

"Well, what do you expect? No humans live here, so it has been preserved," Orion said.

"It kind of reminds me of when I've been in the city a long time and go out to the countryside," Trixie said. "I look around, and I'm surprised how beautiful the natural world can me."

Leo nodded. "Yeah, I get that feeling too… a sense of peace."

"You are returning to your roots," Starla said from her sleeping position. One eye was open and staring at them. "People tend to forget that a long time ago they lived off the land, just like us animals. When you leave the technological world and enter the old world, you cannot help but have a sense of security."

"I guess when you put it that way, you're right." Trixie grinned. "Now enough deep conversations. Let's eat."

It was the middle of the night when Trixie awoke abruptly. The others were still asleep. There was no need to take turns keeping watch since Starla and Orion were never fully asleep.

Trixie took a deep breath, letting the cool air rush over her. She wasn't sure what caused her to wake up, but now she felt too energized to go back to sleep. She closed her eyes for a moment and enjoyed the silence.

"Are you all right, Mera?"

Trixie opened her eyes to see Starla had one eye open. "Yeah, just can't sleep."

Starla opened her other eye and sat up. "Is something wrong?"

Trixie shook her head. "Not really. But there are two things that have been bothering me."

Starla cocked her head to one side as she waited patiently.

"When I was in Quarteze, I could hear the elements talking; but on Earth, even here, I don't hear them."

"The elements here are rather quiet." Starla gazed around the grasslands. "I fear many have become dormant. Similar to what happened to your world, people quit caring and talking to them so they stopped talking." Starla smiled. "Do not worry, Mera. If they wish to talk, they will tell you. Now, what else is bothering you?"

Trixie sighed. "I remember in the Dark Bastion exploring a room filled with designs of sapphire roses. You once said that nothing is coincidental. Could there be a connection between the two; and, if so, why?"

Starla smiled mysteriously. "I did say that." She turned around three times and lay down. "But, there is a belief that, because of the elements, events that happen in one world can affect another world." She sighed. "I do not know if there is a connection. You must find that out on your own." She yawned. "As the saying goes, everything is connected."

"That's what *she* said," Trixie whispered. She glanced at Starla to see she was sleeping again.

She looked at the sky one last time before lying back and closing her eyes.

They had a late start the next morning but tried to make up for it by traveling at a quick pace. By midday, they were sweaty and exhausted. Taking a swig from her canteen, Trixie gazed at the endless sea of tall grass that lay before them. "How much farther until we get there?"

Book, who happened to be in her arms, flipped open. "*We must reach the Seven Falls in order to find the entrance to Shal Ron Lee's library.*"

All four froze when they heard a rustling from their left.

"Can you see what that was?" Starla asked as she glanced in Orion's direction.

Orion frowned. "I can see auras. I cannot see through tall grass."

"You do not have to be so grumpy about it," Starla said under her breath.

Trixie let out a slight yelp as she felt something brush against her leg. Taking a couple of steps back, she found herself facing the creature from Alfred's video feed. The capybara-like creature cocked its head to one side as its feelers reached out to her once more.

"What is that?" Leo said as he raised the Dark Blade in caution.

"*It's a babosa. They feed off the same foods that capybaras eat. They're gentle and shy by nature. Those streamers you see are feelers. They use them to examine their surroundings.*"

Trixie giggled as a feeler brushed against her. "That tickles."

"*This is good. Babosas live near rivers.*"

"I guess that means we head in the direction the babosas came from," Leo said as another babosa appeared beside him. It cocked its head and let out a grunt.

As they walked, they encountered more and more babosas. Within minutes, they reached the river. A babosa and its cub were drinking from the water. Seeing the quartet, they quickly ran off into the tall grass.

"Look, there is a boat tied up over there." Starla pointed to the left with her paw.

Indeed, a medium-size rowboat was bobbing lazily in the water.

"How convenient," Orion said cheerfully.

"Do you think it belongs to someone?" Trixie asked.

Starla's eyes narrowed as she examined the boat. "If it does, they have not used it recently. There is an inch of grime on the bottom."

"Then I highly doubt they will mind if we borrow it," Orion said.

Leo stepped into the boat and tested it. "It feels sturdy."

They piled into the boat. After untying the rope, Leo slowly began to paddle down stream. After a few minutes, the current became stronger. Rounding a corner, the quartet gasped at the sight that lay before them.

"The Seven Falls," Trixie whispered.

Three waterfalls on each side came crashing down into the river. The waterfalls churned the water, causing the boat to rock back and forth violently. They passed so close to a waterfall that Trixie could feel the spray hit her face. The seventh fall lay before them. Unlike its brethren, the churning waters pushed the water up the waterfall into the sky.

"I guess you would call the seventh fall a waterup." Orion said.

Starla slapped her paw against her forehead. "Bad joke, Orion. You need to work on your humor."

Glancing around, Trixie realized that the river ended at the seventh fall.

"Are we supposed to climb that thing?" Leo asked.

"I do believe we have to," Starla said.

Leo held his hand to his forehead and squinted. "Yeah, well, how are we going to do that? Our boat is so heavy that gravity will make us fall back down."

Trixie sighed as she fished through her pack. "Honestly, do I really have to remind you that I can control elements?" She pulled the Harp of Oriantist out and placed it in her lap. Quickly playing the string for water, she focused her thoughts on traveling up the waterfall.

The water churned around the boat. Slowly, the boat started to climb the waterfall. They climbed and climbed. Beads of sweat were beginning to form on her forehead as Trixie began to wonder if the waterfall ever ended.

"Look," Orion said.

Trixie opened her eyes. Before them was a large gray castle. It seemed to sit on the clouds itself. If Trixie hadn't noticed the propellers rotating at the bottom, she might have believed it. A large wooden pier at the edge of the waterfall led to the castle.

Starla smiled. "Mera, gentlemen, I do believe we have reached our destination."

Chapter 14:

SHAL RON LEE

As everyone stepped out, Leo quickly tied the boat to the pier. It was cool, and a strong breeze whipped by occasionally. The only sounds were the creaking of the pier and the dull roar of the waterfalls down below.

"Well, shall we?" Orion asked as he fidgeted impatiently.

"After you." Leo bowed towards Trixie.

Trixie laughed as she walked by. "Show off."

Within minutes, they reached the front doors. Leo was about to reach out and knock when the doors opened inward.

Leo raised an eyebrow as he looked back at them.

"It seems we are expected," Starla said.

"It seems so," Trixie added.

Orion groaned. "Let us go in already. We will not find out anything just standing here." He quickly passed Leo.

"What's his rush?" Leo asked.

Starla and Trixie shrugged as they followed Orion inside.

Orion was standing in the center of the room, his eyes as big as saucers.

Looking around, the other three gasped.

"Whoa," Trixie said.

"That is what I said," Orion added.

Every inch of the walls were covered by shelves of books that seemed to stretch forever, both horizontal and vertical; and there was also a maze of standing shelves that lay before them.

"This guy must have a lot of time on his hands," Leo said.

"That or he is a little obsessed with books," Orion said as he shook his head. A hooting sound caused them to look upward. A great horned owl was perched on one of the higher shelves. As it watched the quartet closely, it let out another hoot, which was immediately echoed by other hoots. Glancing around, Trixie saw that there were many owls roosting on the shelves. They ranged from the common barn owl to the rare spotted owl. All of them were gazing at the quartet.

"Okay, I am slightly weirded out by the staring contest," Trixie whispered.

"Yeah, I'm really not liking the freaky owl stares," Leo whispered back.

"Well, what do you expect?" Starla said. "We have invaded their home. Of course they are going to be hesitant."

"Why are they staring at us?" Leo shifted from one foot to the other. "Are we supposed to talk to them? Can they even talk?"

Orion laughed. "Animals are a lot smarter than humans give them credit for." He smirked as he gazed at the owls. "Hey, do any of you know where we can find the spirit known as Shal Ron Lee?"

His reply was a chorus of hoots. A burrowing owl left its roost and descended. Hovering above them, the owl hooted once before zooming down one of the aisles. Without hesitation, the quartet followed.

For five minutes, the owl led them through the maze of shelves, only stopping a couple of times to allow them to catch up. The chase finally ended at a large opening in the middle of the maze of shelves. A couple of desks and chairs were placed randomly as a fire burned in the fireplace to the left of them. The owl hooted happily as it perched itself on a chair near the fire. It ruffled its feather and slowly closed its eyes.

"I guess we're here," Trixie said after she caught her breath. "Wherever here is."

"Dang that bird is fast," Leo said as he leaned heavily against a bookcase. "I mean, did you see it zip around those shelves?"

"Hmm." Orion surveyed the area with curiosity. "I wonder where Shal Ron Lee is."

"He should be nearby." Starla sniffed the air. "I smell a scent that is definitely not owl."

"That is because I am not an avian," said a voice from the shadows. "I am from the canine family."

A figure emerged from the shadows. A giant red fox stood before them. It had intelligent green eyes, sharp white teeth, and nine tails.

Amused by their expressions, the fox grinned. "Please permit me to introduce myself. I am known as Shal Ron Lee, the keeper of knowledge."

"You're a fox," Leo said. "I thought you would be a giant owl or something."

"In my world, we have a country known as Japan," Trixie said. "Their mythology states that foxes are clever and wise. They believe that the wisest fox is one that has nine tails." She smiled at Shal Ron Lee. "I assume this same belief exists in Orcania?"

"You are correct, little one," Shal Ron Lee said. "That same belief exists in our world." He stretched his legs before sitting down. "It is astounding that such petite creatures could cause my searchers so much anxiety."

"Searchers?" Leo asked.

"The owls," Shal Ron Lee said. "They are my gatherers of knowledge. I maintain this dwelling while they inquire about new information." He paused as he studied the quartet. "But I do believe this visit isn't about pleasantries."

"We need to find the Sapphire Rose before Dirdrom, a man who wishes to take over Orcania, does," Trixie said.

Shal Ron Lee's face remained expressionless. "I have heard of him."

We were told you would know where the rose is." Trixie pulled out the lullaby bloom while Leo pulled out the purple scallop. "We were told by Gardenia and Aquaritus to give these to you."

"Let me see them." Shal Ron Lee took the items from Leo and Trixie. He sniffed them slightly. "These items have their scent." He set them aside and looked at the quartet. "Yes, I do know the whereabouts of the Sapphire Rose."

The quartet's faces lit up.

"The information you need lies in a book behind this shelf." Shal Ron Lee pointed to the bookshelf to their right. It was against a wall.

"There's nothing behind there but a wall," Leo said.

Shal Ron Lee grinned. "Ah, you are perceiving it as you see it. Look closer."

Trixie and Leo squinted at the shelf. The shelves were color coordinated by spines. A red book was placed within a section of blue, while a blue book was placed in a section of red. Trixie and Leo looked at each other before grabbing the misplaced books and putting them in their correct positions.

A loud rumbling sound filled the room as the shelf moved to the side revealing a hidden room. In the middle of the room was a desk. A blue book with roses delicately drawn on the cover lay on the desk.

"Hm," Shal Ron Lee said as he walked past them. "It seems you have passed the first test."

"Wait, you're testing us?" Leo asked.

"You didn't honestly expect me to simply give you the answer," Shal Ron Lee said. "You must be tested to see if you are worthy of receiving the knowledge." He glanced at Orion and Starla. "Plus, your comrades over there cannot help."

Orion looked as if he were about to protest when Starla held up her paw and shook her head. "We understand. We will do what is needed to learn the whereabouts of the rose."

Satisfied, Shal Ron Lee grabbed the book with one of his tails. He took it from his tail before looking at Leo and Trixie. "All right, I have one more question to ask you." He grinned slightly. "It's rather simple, really. If you answer correctly, I will give the book to you. If you answer incorrectly, you must leave my domain at once." He paused for effect. "Simply, tell me who you are."

Leo raised an eyebrow while Trixie's eyes widened.

Leo crossed his arms. "Why are you asking us this?"

Shal Ron Lee sat on his haunches. "Because, in order to understand where the Sapphire Rose is, you need to let go of the normal perceptions of the world."

"Wait," she frowned. "What do you mean by who we are? Are you talking about our names and appearances or our heritage? Both contribute to who we are."

Shal Ron Lee laughed. "Hm, you are a clever human. Perhaps, I should rephrase my question. I want you to tell me who you truly are, not how others perceive you." He motioned to his left. "You may look in the mirror if you need an aide."

Trixie and Leo traded confused glances before walking toward the standing mirror. It was old with gold scallops framing the edge. As they peered in the mirror, all they saw were their images staring back.

"If we see us as we are, that means we are seeing ourselves as others see us, right?" Trixie asked.

Shal Ron Lee's lips quirked. "Maybe, or maybe that is how you truly are."

"How do you know if we're describing our real selves?" Leo asked. "We could lie to you."

Shal Ron Lee laughed. "One of the perks of being enlightened is that you are able to perceive others' true selves." He stared at them, unblinking. "In other words, I will know if you are lying."

Trixie and Leo turned their attention to the mirror. She furrowed her brow in concentration as she stared at her image. How was she supposed to see her true self when she didn't even know what her true self looked like? She closed her eyes and took a couple of deep breaths. She cleared her mind and focused her thoughts on the image in the mirror. She knew she was an avid reader. That was an important part of her. It represented her quest for knowledge. She was definitely adventurous. Why else would she be on this adventure, trying to figure out who she was? Also, she was loyal and loving. She didn't know what she would do if something were to happen to her friends and family. Satisfied with what she had discovered, she decided to look in the mirror.

When she opened her eyes again, she let out a gasp. The image of herself had been replaced by a younger version. She wore a white dress and held a book in her hand. In her lap was a little white dog. Both of them looked at her with triumphant grins.

"What do you see?" Shal Ron Lee asked from behind her, startling her.

"I see a younger version of myself." Trixie watched the image in the mirror. "I'm probably six or seven. I'm wearing a white dress, and in my hands is a book. Also, a little white dog is sitting in my lap."

"Darn it," Shal Ron Lee took a couple of steps away from them.

Leo smirked. "She's right; isn't she?"

Shal Ron Lee growled. "You weren't supposed to answer correctly. No one has ever been able to answer correctly."

"A deal is a deal," Orion said. "We held up our end of the bargain. Now it is time for you to uphold your end."

Shal Ron Lee sighed. "Fine." He opened the book and quickly skimmed the pages. Finding what he was looking for, he cleared his throat and said, "Here it is." He handed the book to Leo. Trixie, Starla, and Orion peered over his shoulder as they read:

In its petals, it holds life
And in its thorns, it holds death.
The paradox lies where the three graces of humanity meet.
There shall it forever remain, protected by its own power
And only will it be removed again by a virgin's touch.

"It's a riddle," Leo said, frustration evident in his voice. "We asked for the location, not a riddle."

"Well, if you were wise enough, you would see that the location was in the riddle." Shal Ron Lee shrugged. "It is not my fault you cannot understand it."

Trixie was about to protest when he quickly cut her off. "Ah!" He held up a claw. "As you said, a deal's a deal. I held up my end of the bargain, so now it is time for you to uphold yours."

The room began to spin round and round making her feel nauseous. When it finally stopped, they found themselves in the grasslands once more.

Chapter 15:

NIGHTMARES ON THE TRAVEL BUS

IT took the quartet a couple of minutes before finally accepting that they would not be able to return to Shal Ron Lee's library.

"I guess our next step is to figure out where we are and find our way back to the Torac's camp," Leo said with a sigh. "We have nowhere else to go."

"Maybe they can figure out what the riddle means," Trixie added.

Book flipped open in her hands. *"As luck would have it, Shal Ron Lee has transported us to the other side of the grasslands. Which means we don't have to go back the way we came."*

"So, we don't have to go through the null void zone?" Trixie asked, relief flooding into her voice.

"Yes, our best bet is to travel to the end of the grasslands to the earth region. There we will take the travel bus to Srilo village where a kadir will take us to the Torac's camp." On the opposite page, Book drew a map of the route they would be taking.

"Well," Starla said, "if we are all in agreement, then let us go!"

They traveled a fair amount of distance before night fell. Exhausted, they kept to themselves as they settled down to sleep. Trixie's mind was abuzz as she spread her blanket. It seemed as if no matter how hard she tried, the riddle kept bugging her. She felt that the answer was on the tip of her tongue. So, it was no surprise that she was still awake long after the others had fallen asleep. Letting out a sigh, she sat up and looked around. The rustle of the wind through the grasslands was relaxing. She froze as she heard faint singing.

"The night is young as I sing my joyful loving melody," a voice sang, "The crickets chirp, the owls hoot, and the wolves howl as they take their much needed bow."

"Plue?" Trixie called as happiness rushed over her. "Is that you?"

"The night is young as I sing my joyful loving melody," the voice continued to sing as it slowly faded away. "The crickets chirp, the owls hoot, and the wolves howl. All to my melody."

Trixie sighed. It was no use calling again. The owner of the voice had already left.

"You still up?" Leo yawned as he sat up.

She looked back at him. "Yeah, I thought I heard Plue; but it must have been my imagination."

Leo sat beside her. "Well, it's possible that you heard him; but he could have been miles away." Leo tossed a twig into the fire. "You don't know what spirits are capable of."

Trixie nodded. "I suppose…"

They were silent for a couple of moments.

"So," Leo leaned back onto the palms of his hands. "I don't know about you, but I am so glad we aren't going through the null void again."

Trixie smirked. "You probably would be okay. Me, on the other hand, I couldn't handle it."

Leo frowned. "What do you mean?"

Trixie looked down at her feet. "Even without magic, you can take care of yourself. You're a master of the sword. That comes naturally to you." Trixie drew a line in the dirt with her shoe. "Me, I'm only good when I can use magic. Without it, I'm useless." Trixie looked away. "I never realized how useless I can be."

She stiffened slightly when she felt a hand on her shoulder. Leo smiled. "You're not useless. You never were. What you can't do in strength, you make up with in knowledge."

"You… really believe that?" Trixie asked hesitantly.

Leo nodded. "I know it."

She gave Leo a hug. "Thanks, Leo. You can always cheer me up."

Leo blushed slightly as he hugged her back. "No problem."

"Psst," Orion whispered. "Mara, tell her that she completes you."

Both Trixie and Leo turned bright red as they looked back at Orion. With her eyes still shut, Starla whacked Orion on the back of the head. "Shh! You are supposed to be sleeping."

"You're both awake?" Leo rubbed the bridge of his nose.

Starla opened her eyes as they both grinned sheepishly. "You know that neither one of us needs to sleep in order to regain energy."

"Don't tell me everyone was listening to our conversation." Trixie glanced down at Book. "At least Book is asleep."

Book quickly flipped open. *"Oh no, I never sleep."*

"I'm going to bed." Leo got up, dusted his pants, and walked back to his blanket.

"Me too," Trixie added as she sent a glare in Starla's and Orion's direction.

"Geez." Orion yawned. "Why are humans so touchy?"

The next morning they awoke early and set out. It was midday when they reached the earth region. It was strange seeing the two regions side by side. The earth region looked parched and devoid of plant life compared to the lush grasslands. The earth region also lacked different colors or life. In fact, the only difference in the rocky orange region was a random blue sign stuck in the ground.

The quartet approached the sign.

"This is so random," Trixie said as she ran her finger down its silver pole. "What's it doing here?"

"I do believe," Starla sniffed the air, "that this is where we wait for the bus."

A rumbling sound approached from the left. Glancing in that direction, Trixie saw a huge cloud of sand approaching them.

"Oh boy." Leo rubbed his forehead with the back of his hand. "A sandstorm's about to hit."

"That is no sandstorm." Orion chuckled. "I do believe that is our ride."

Moments later, the sound of screeching brakes was heard as the cloud of sand engulfed them. They coughed as they tried to fan the sand away. When their vision cleared, they found themselves standing at the door of a large, red double-decker bus. On its side, painted in fancy gold letters, were the words Travel Bus.

The door squealed as it opened. A portly young man stepped out. He wore the traditional bus driver's garb, consisting of a white collared shirt and dark blue pants. He also had a matching captain's hat. Red hair peeked from under the visor. His blue eyes squinted as he looked over the quartet. Grinning sheepishly, he said, "Sorry about that. We're still trying to invent a way to prevent sandstorms from forming around us."

"That's fine." Trixie coughed, "So, you're the travel bus?"

The bus driver beamed. "The one and only. We're the fastest mode of transportation in all of Orcania." He jerked his thumb towards himself. "I'm Gibbs. So, how can I be of service to you today?"

"Can you take us to Srilo Village?" Leo asked.

Gibbs nodded. "But of course." He quickly eyeballed the quartet. "Just pay ten quarpos, and you'll be set."

"I think I still have some money left that Jamul gave me." Leo fished through his pack. His face lit up as he pulled out a few bills and gave them to Gibbs. "Will that suffice?"

Gibbs thumbed through the bills. "Yep, that'll do it. Hop aboard."

They quickly boarded the bus. Glancing around, Trixie noted that many of the passengers looked like farmers. One old woman was even holding a piglet in her lap. Finding four seats, they quickly sat down.

Gibbs tipped his hat before settling into the driver's seat. He honked the horn once before pulling out. The bus jerked, and then they were off.

It was twilight when the bus stopped for a break. Gibbs allowed everyone to have a stretch break while he refueled. Trixie let out a contented sigh as she stretched her arms. She was glad to have a chance to loosen up her muscles.

Letting her hands drop, Trixie took a moment to take in her surroundings. The expanse before them was littered with rocks; and, less than a mile away, she could see a herd of horses. Their coats were jet black, and their eyes glowed neon green. Most had their heads down as they grazed, but there were a couple who were watching the small crowd around the travel bus. Trixie shivered at the intensity of their stares.

She frowned. "Those are strange horses. I wonder what they are?"

Book rustled from within her pack. She pulled it out, and it flipped open. "*They're night mares. Their name is a double entendre since herds mostly consist of nocturnal females. It is said that if you look one in the eye, you will have nightmares. The males generally live solitary lives.*"

"They give you nightmares, huh?" She glanced back at the herd. A young filly left the herd and walked toward the bus. Her head was cocked curiously as she eyed the group. When her gaze met the filly's, Trixie felt drawn into the filly's eyes.

All she could see was green. After a moment, a scene began to form in the green haze.

She was lying on the floor of a small room with no windows. Her whole body ached as her vision blurred in and out of focus. Incoherent murmuring was heard, and she found herself shaking her head. Pain bit into her back as a scream threatened to rip through her lips.

Once more, she heard the incoherent murmuring; and, once again, she shook her head. She heard the sound of a whip cracking as pain raced through her body. Gasping and sobbing, she felt a hand slowly turn her face toward her attacker.

"Glade," a voice whispered. For half a second, the face of her attacker was illuminated; but that second was ended as a loud roaring sound filled her ears.

Trixie blinked as she shook her head. An old woman was standing in front of her. She had the piglet under one arm and a revolver in the other hand. "Shambalay!" she yelled as she fired into the air once more.

The night mares shrieked as they quickly retreated from the bus.

Trixie felt something bump her hand. "Mera?" Starla asked. "Are you all right?"

Trixie shook her head. "What happened?"

"You tell me." Leo crossed his arms.

"One minute you were fine, and the next you were frozen like a statue," Orion added.

"Night mares," the old woman returned the revolver back to the holster on her waist. "Bad."

Trixie nodded. "I think I was having a nightmare."

Starla frowned. "What of?"

Trixie shook her head again. "I think I was having a nightmare about Glade."

"Of Glade?" Leo said.

"Hey!" Gibbs yelled as he ran toward them. "No guns! There are no weapons on this bus."

The woman frowned in confusion for a second. She shrugged as she boarded the bus. Gibbs massaged his temples. "Why me?" With a sigh, he motioned to the other passengers. "The bus is ready to go. All aboard!"

As Trixie boarded the bus, many thoughts ran through her mind. She was positive that the nightmare the filly showed her was what was happening to Glade. If her hunch was correct, her attacker had to be Dirdrom. She frowned as she replayed the images through her mind. Although she could not remember the face of her attacker, she did remember experiencing déjà vu, which she knew could only mean one thing.

I must have already met or seen Dirdrom, she thought as the bus slowly began to move. *And I didn't even realize it.*

Chapter 16:

SRILO VILLAGE

IT was the following day when Srilo village appeared on the horizon. A line of horse-drawn carriages and cars were lined up at the entrance. Gibbs frowned as he rubbed the back of his head. "What the heck is going on here?"

Everyone pressed their faces against the windows for a better look. The bus eased slowly toward the entrance; and, after a minute, a man wearing a black uniform approached the bus. His face was hardened and his expression stern as he watched the bus. He motioned to Gibbs to open the door and then stepped into the bus. Glancing over the passengers, the man said, "This is a routine check. We'll have you through in a couple of minutes."

Leo leaned toward Trixie's ear and whispered, "Man, security is tight here."

"I know," Trixie whispered back. "I wonder why."

Uniformed men forced everyone to open their bags so they could see their contents. When they came to the old woman, she stared at them defiantly.

"Aha!" one of the officers said as he snatched the revolver from her holster. "It is illegal to carry weapons in Srilo. This will have to come with us."

Furious, the woman began to ramble in a different language. The officer snickered and cuffed her.

"She doesn't understand," Gibbs said as he pointed to the hysterical woman.

The commanding officer shrugged. "Not my fault. Any weapons will be confiscated, and failure to cooperate, in any language," he glanced back at the woman, "will get you arrested."

Leo grasped Trixie's wrist. She frowned in confusion. "My sword," he hissed. Trixie's eyes widened. The Dark Blade would be confiscated. It was too big for him to hide.

The commanding officer cleared his throat as he eyed the sword. "Okay, hand it over."

Leo placed a hand protectively over the hilt of the sword. "We're only staying here for a night. Can I get it back when we leave?"

The man remained expressionless as he held out his hand. "All weapons will be confiscated and will stay confiscated. Those are the rules. And if you don't comply..." All eyes turned to the old woman being dragged off the bus.

Resigned, Leo handed over the Dark Blade. The officer eyed the sword curiously before motioning the other officers to leave.

Once they were out of earshot, Trixie whispered, "Don't worry, we'll get it back."

Leo shook his head. "That's not what I'm worried about." Seeing Trixie's confusion, he added, "The Dark Blade is an enchanted object. Enchanted objects sometimes act life-like."

Trixie grimaced as she imagined the sword springing to life in the officer's hands.

About thirty minutes later, they finally managed to get into the city. The city itself was dark and dingy. A streetlamp buzzed and flickered off and on to their right. A couple of tumbleweeds rolled lazily around the dirt streets.

One by one the passengers exited the travel bus. Orion and Starla remained silent, pretending to be ordinary animals. Gibbs stood by the door bidding them goodbye. Trixie could tell that he was still upset over the old woman's arrest. *I am, too,* she thought. *It seems all of Orcania has gone paranoid.*

Trixie sighed as she collapsed on a bed. They scrounged enough money for one night at a cheap motel. Leo had gone out to see if he could find where they were keeping the confiscated weapons. Each minute he was gone, the more anxious Trixie became. She wasn't sure why, but she felt as if something terrible was about to happen.

Trixie rubbed her forehead as she surveyed the room in dismay. The room was dingy, and she was sure she saw a couple of roaches scurry to the cover of the shadows when she flicked on the solitary overhead light. When she sat on the bed, a couple of dust balls bounced off; and she was overwhelmed with the smell of mildew. But none of them cared. They weren't planning to spend the night.

"Ugh," Orion said as he stretched his body. "I hate having to act like I am stupid. Not being able to talk is a pain."

"We need a plan," Trixie said as she anxiously stared out the window.

Starla sighed. "We cannot do any planning until Leo returns."

The door opened, and Leo walked in. He looked both ways before closing the door. "Okay, I found where they are holding the confiscated weapons. It's on the other side of town and has tight security, but I think we can do it."

"So," Orion licked his paw as he washed himself, "what are we going to do?"

"I will acquire a kadir while you three get the Dark Blade," Starla said.

Orion placed his paw down and glared. "Wait, how come you get to acquire the kadir?"

"Because," Starla grinned as she pranced over to Trixie, "I am better at it than you."

Before they could get into an argument again, Trixie said, "So, let's plan how we're going to get the Dark Blade."

It had just turned dark when Trixie, Leo and Orion arrived at the building where the confiscated weapons were housed. Looking at it closely, it resembled an oversized scout post. It was wooden and simple in design. It had four windows and only one door. Squinting through the darkness, Trixie could barely see two guards standing out front.

"We need a plan to distract them," Leo whispered.

"Leave that to me." Orion winked as he slinked into the darkness.

Trixie and Leo glanced at each other nervously. Moments later, Orion's voice drifted toward them.

"Ooohhhhh," Orion moaned, causing the two guards to peer cautiously through the darkness. "Ooohhhh."

"Who's there?" one of the guards yelled.

"I am the ghost of a victim of the black leopard," Orion said in a ghostly voice. "I was killed unjustly and now must wander Orcania forever."

"Stop joking around, whoever you are." The other guard waved his gun around. "We'll arrest you for this nonsense."

"Beware the black leopard," Orion said. "Or you could end up like me, too." He appeared in front of them. The guards stiffened as they dropped their guns. Orion growled, and the guards screamed as they ran away. Orion let out a cackle as he chased after them.

Trixie blinked, unable to process what had happened.

Leo smacked his forehead. "I guess we should take advantage of the distraction."

Trixie and Leo slipped through the door and cautiously moved through the halls, intently listening for any guards. Trixie was about to round a corner when Leo reached out and grabbed her shoulder. She opened her mouth to ask him why, when he covered it and pointed ahead of her. Looking up, Trixie realized that a security camera was trained on the hallway in front of them. She could hear its motorized engine running as the camera swiveled back and forth. With the stark white walls of the hallway, there was no way they could pass the camera without being seen.

Leo removed his hand from her mouth and whispered, "we need to change its direction."

"I've got an idea." Trixie pulled the Harp of Oriantist out from her pack. She quickly struck the string that summoned wind. Focusing on the camera, she willed the wind upward. Slowly the camera began to turn upward until it was facing the ceiling.

"Nice," Leo said.

Trixie pretended to brush dust off her shoulder. "It was nothing." She tucked the harp back in her pack.

After a few minutes, the hall dead-ended at a glass room. Peering around the corner, Trixie noted rotating security cameras all around the halls. There were a couple of officers in the glass room. They were leaning back in wooden chairs as they idly flipped through magazines. A large wooden table lined the back wall. Lying on the table with a white tag attached to it was the Dark Blade.

"How are we going to get the Dark Blade without them noticing?" Trixie asked.

Leo's face lit up as he pointed to the far left corner. "You see that plant over there? Do you think you can control it from here?"

Trixie followed Leo's finger to a small houseplant sitting in the corner. "I think so," Trixie said as she produced the harp from her pack. "Here goes." She immediately played the string that summoned the plants. She focused on the plant. Slowly the plant's vines began to grow. Unnoticed by the guards, the vines slithered across the table until they reached the Dark Blade. They quickly wrapped themselves around the blade and began to drag it across the table.

Leo gave her a thumbs up while Trixie grinned.

As the vines slid past a knife, they accidentally brushed it causing the knife to hit the floor with a loud clang. Both guards looked up.

The guard on the left gaped at the vines. "What the—"

"Shoot," Leo said.

In distress, Trixie sent all of her energy into the vines. The vines raised up and threw the Dark Blade through the glass wall. The sword crashed through the wall sending shards of glass everywhere. Leo quickly scrambled forward and grabbed the sword while the guards stood frozen.

Relieved, Trixie rushed to help him and stumbled; but Leo caught her before she fell.

"You okay?" Leo asked as he pulled her to her feet.

Trixie nodded as she regained her footing. "Yeah, just a little exhausted from using all that magic."

With clinched fists, one of the guards shouted. "Get them!"

Leo grabbed her wrist and dragged her after him.

They quickly ran down the halls. It was taking a long time for Trixie, and the halls seemed to blur together. She knew this was from her fatigue, but she couldn't help but wonder if they had stumbled into a strange white-walled maze with no escape. These thoughts were banished when Leo threw the door open, and she was greeted by the cool night air.

"Hold it right there," an officer pointed his gun at them. They both froze with their hands up. "Now, slowly turn around."

Trixie and Leo looked at each other before slowly turning around. The two guards had guns pointed at them

"What can we do?" Trixie whispered.

"Don't move," the other guard said.

An explosion went off behind them. The force knocked them a couple of feet forward.

Trixie groaned as she rubbed the back of her head. "What happened?" Her eyes widened as she stood up. "Leo? Are you okay?"

Leo groaned as he too stood up. "Yeah, what happened?"

Orion appeared in front of them. "Come on. We have to get out of here. Srilo is under attack."

Trixie snapped her head towards Orion. "What?"

"Who's attacking?" Leo added.

Orion shrugged. "I am not sure. I have heard it is the Toracs."

"What?" Leo and Trixie said in unison.

Orion shifted from one foot to the other. "No time to talk. Let us go."

As they ran, Trixie watched in horror as masked men clad entirely in black were setting buildings on fire and causing explosions. They reminded Trixie of animated shadows as they destroyed anything they came in contact with. People were screaming as they tried to dodge the destruction. *This couldn't be caused by the Toracs,* Trixie thought as she forced her attention back to following her companions. *They wouldn't cause so much damage and hurt so many innocent people.*

After a few minutes, they entered the kadir docking area.

"Come on," Starla yelled as she jumped up and down. "Let us get out of here."

To the right, Trixie saw that Starla already had the kadir ready to go. A vent was sitting in the crow's nest watching them curiously.

Without hesitation, Orion, Trixie, and Leo joined Starla on the kadir. Leo signaled the vent to go. Taking a deep breath, the vent began to blow, moving the kadir. As they slowly left Srilo village, Trixie couldn't help but look back. A wave of sadness washed over her as she watched the village crumble to the ground, illuminated by the orange flames licking at the night sky.

Chapter 17:

EPIPHANY

T HE trip back to the Toracs' camp was a silent one. None of the quartet was eager to talk. After the destruction they had just witnessed and the accusations they heard, they were suffering from a mixture of stupor and sadness.

No one wanted to believe that the Toracs had anything to do with what happened in Srilo. There was always a chance that someone had set them up or maybe the Toracs really did attack Srilo to spite the High Council. They knew, though, that the only way they were going to get answers were from the Toracs themselves.

Luckily, fate was with them; because they did not encounter any sand sharks during the night. As dawn approached, they could see the outlineof the Toracs' campsite on the horizon.

Leo watched Trixie as she leaned heavily against the kadir. There were dark circles under her eyes, and she kept yawning. "You okay?"

She nodded as she forced herself to stand up. "Yeah." She looked back toward the campsite. "I guess we'll find out if they really did it or not."

After a few minutes, Starla lifted her nose to the air. Orion frowned before lifting his as well.

"What's wrong?" Trixie asked.

"Something is burning," Starla said as her gaze drifted towards Trixie.

Orion nodded. "I believe it is coming from the campsite." A feeling of foreboding filled the quartet as they approached the Toracs.

Once the kadir was parked and the vent tended to, Trixie found herself gasping at the campsite. Scorch marks were everywhere and a couple of piles that were once tents were still smoldering. The Toracs were dirty and ragged. Their disposition, dispirited. The children huddled together as they mournfully watched the world pass by. The adults wandered aimlessly, picking up items here and there. Their faces were drawn tight from exhaustion and anxiety.

It took them a few minutes before they found Jamul. Calypso and he were busy directing a crowd of people to different jobs. Seeing the quartet, Jamul smiled, a smile Trixie noticed that seemed forced. As they approached, Calypso discreetly directed lollygaggers away from Jamul's vicinity.

"Please tell me you've found the Sapphire Rose," Jamul whispered.

Leo shook his head sadly. "We haven't found the rose, but we have found a clue to its whereabouts."

"If only we could figure it out," Trixie said under her breath.

Jamul's face fell. "Ah, I was hoping for better news." He watched his comrades as they slowly cleaned the area. "Something to cheer them up." Jamul looked left and right before leaning towards them. "Did you hear about what happened in Srilo?"

Orion laughed. "Hear about it? We were in it."

"We didn't see who caused it though," Trixie quickly added.

Jamul pinched the bridge of his nose. "Well, it seems that they are blaming it on us. We couldn't have possibly organized such an assault at this time. After I left you, we were attacked two more times by masked men clad entirely in black. I bet they are responsible for the attack in Srilo as well." He ran his fingers through his hair. "And the worst part is that the High Council has enough evidence to try and evict us."

"Couldn't you contest it?" Trixie asked. "They may reconsider if you explain what has been happening."

Jamul shook his head. "They won't believe us. None of them trust us." His face lit up. "But, they might trust you."

"Us?" Leo asked.

"But we aren't credible witnesses," Trixie said. "We never saw who attacked."

"It doesn't matter." Jamul said. "You two are magic users. People listen to magic users. If you were to tell them what is going on right now with us, they may reconsider evicting us."

Trixie glanced at Starla who shrugged. "It is Leo's and your choice, Mera."

"Well," Trixie began, "I guess we could try…"

Jamul looked relieved. "Oh, thank you so much. And when you get back, I promise we will help you figure out the clue to the Sapphire Rose."

The kadir ride was relatively smooth; and, before they knew it, they were back in Crangor City. After tying the kadir to a post, the quartet slowly walked to the High Council's headquarters.

Unlike before, Trixie could sense the tension in the air. There were no kids taking the dolphin cabs for joy rides, and everyone seemed to watch them with distrust.

Leo leaned towards her. "I guess what happened in Srilo is scaring everyone."

Trixie nodded.

Once they reached the headquarters, they immediately went to the receptionist's desk. The receptionist directed them to some chairs and asked them to wait. Looking around, Trixie noted how busy everyone seemed. People were running around, their arms full of documents, while others were busy at their desks. It was almost chaotic.

"There is going to be a war soon," Orion whispered.

Starla nodded. "Yes, tension is too high. They only need one more straw to break the camel's back."

They all knew what that one straw was.

After a few minutes, the receptionist asked for them to follow her. As they walked, Trixie realized from her previous visit that they were being taken to the throne room. *I wonder why they are taking us there?* she thought, as the receptionist opened the door.

She peeked her head inside and said. "They are here." She quickly pulled her head back and opened the door all the way. "He is ready to see you."

Trixie and Leo looked at each other, the same thought running through both of their heads. He? Didn't she mean they?

As the quartet walked into the room, the receptionist closed the door. Trixie was surprised to see Mordrid standing before them.

"Hello, Trixie," Mordrid took her hand in his and kissed it. He said a gruff hello to Leo before continuing. "I am the one you will be speaking with today."

Leo raised an eyebrow. "They sent *you* to talk to us?"

Mordrid turned and raised an eyebrow as well. "The Toracs sent a little boy to plead their case?"

"So, you know why we're here," Trixie said, hoping to prevent an altercation.

"Yes," Mordrid sat down on the throne. "But I doubt what you have to say will do any good. However, I am willing to listen."

"Look," Trixie said. "The Toracs couldn't have caused the attack in Srilo. They have been cleaning up the damage caused by a group of masked people clothed in black."

"Have you seen..." Leo began.

"How do you know that it wasn't something they staged so that they could have an alibi?" Mordrid asked as he propped his head with his hand.

"We don't," Trixie paused. "But we know them."

"And," Leo added, "we saw the damage at Srilo. They couldn't have possibly..."

"Did you see who caused the destruction?" Mordrid asked.

"We saw masked men clad in black," Trixie said. "The same men that the Toracs described who attacked their campsite."

"Were you able to identify their faces?" Mordrid asked.

Trixie and Leo shook their heads.

"Then how do you know that the Toracs didn't do it?"

Silence filled the room. Trixie knew that they had no evidence to prove the Toracs' innocence.

After a moment, Mordrid stood up. "Look, I know what you are going through. You've probably become friends with them, but you see what the High Council is going through. We would like to think they are innocent, but we can't be sure." He paused. "However, since you seem to believe that they are trustworthy, I will see if I can put in a good word for them."

"Thank you, Mordrid," Trixie said. "We really appreciate this."

Mordrid kissed her hand once again. "Any time, my dear."

Once they were out of earshot, Leo let out a deep breath.

"Something up, Mara?" Orion asked.

"I just don't trust that guy." Leo crossed his arms. "There's just something...off about him."

"But he helped us," Trixie added. "That has got to count for something."

"Maybe." Leo placed his arms behind his head. "But isn't it strange that the son of the supposed leader of the High Council met with us but not one of the council members? It seems like something they would be interested in."

"But he did say they were away," Trixie said. "Isn't it better that we were seen by someone?"

"I suppose," Leo's frown deepened. "But why does he think he has influence on the council? He is just the leader's son."

Trixie sighed. "Oh, come on. You don't seriously think he is evil?"

"I agree with Leo on this one, Mera," Starla said as she trotted beside her. "The boy may have saved your life, but there is something off about him."

They were silent the rest of the way to the kadir. Trixie was still upset over the accusations of her new friend.

He couldn't possibly be evil...could he? She thought. Letting that thought slide, her thoughts drifted to the whereabouts of the Sapphire Rose. As she gazed back at Crangor City, she could barely discern the outline of the Three Graces Statue. Her eyes widened as a thought occurred her. "Oh my gosh!" Ignoring her friends' confused looks, she quickly pulled Book out and said, "Book what was the riddle Shal Ron Lee gave us?"

"In its petals, it holds life
And in its thorns, it holds death.
The paradox lies where the three graces of humanity meet.
There shall it forever remain, protected by its own power
And only will it be removed again by a virgin's touch."

As she read it, she laughed. "I can't believe it. It's been right under our noses this entire time."

Leo frowned. "What has?"

A huge grin spread across her face. "I know where the Sapphire Rose is."

Chapter 18:

BETRAYAL

"**A**RE you serious?" Leo said with a laugh. "The Sapphire Rose is where the Three Graces Statue is?"

They had waited to discuss Trixie's epiphany until they returned to the Toracs' camp. Once they were settled in their tent with dinner, Trixie told them.

"I know," Trixie said as she played with a strand of her hair. "It's crazy, but that has to be where it is. It makes perfect sense." She turned to Book. "What do you think?"

"There are no other places on Orcania that I know of that fit so perfectly with the riddle."

"If that is where the Sapphire Rose is," Orion said, "then we will have to sneak in tonight. The citizens of Crangor aren't too fond of us right now."

News had spread quickly that they had sided with the Toracs. When they were leaving, they had noticed the glares of the citizens.

"We need a plan." Starla peered outside of the tent. "However, I think it would be wise not to mention what we know to the Toracs yet."

They all silently agreed. None were sure how the Toracs would react if they found out that the Sapphire Rose was so close.

Around midnight, the quartet crept out of their tent. The campsite was quiet since most of the Toracs were sleeping. They quietly made their way to the kadirs. As luck would have it, Gnorf, the original vent they used, was nestled in the crow's nest of one of the kadirs. When Leo poked him, Gnorf blearily opened his eyes. Seeing them, his eyes widened in recognition. He was about to yelp in excitement when Leo quickly fed him some food while Trixie placed her finger to her lips. Gnorf got the message and quietly ate his food. Once everyone was situated, Leo told Gnorf their destination. Without hesitation, Gnorf started up the kadir.

They knew they were taking the risk of encountering a sand shark, so they kept their attention focused on the desert.

After awhile, Crangor City came into sight. Upon arriving, they docked the kadir and slowly slinked into the darkness. The streets were quiet. Trixie glanced at a nearby flyer and realized why. Apparently, a curfew had been set.

"We're breaking curfew," Trixie whispered amused. "I feel like a rebel."

Leo grinned. "Kind of invigorating, isn't it?"

Starla and Orion made a shushing sound. Meekly, they quickly followed.

After a few minutes, they finally reached the center of the city. The Three Graces stood off to their far right. They looked rather mysterious in the pale moonlight.

Leo circled the statue a couple of times before saying, "I don't think there is anything behind it. There might be something under it, but we would have to find a way to move it." He looked at the others. "Any suggestions?"

"Look for a switch," Starla began to sniff around the base of the statue.

"Why would someone put a switch on a statue if they are trying to protect the rose?" Trixie asked as she peered at the face of one of the graces.

"Because," Orion pawed at the base. "Someone had to have tended to it. It is a rose after all. The caretaker is probably long dead, but I bet they left a way to get inside so that others could take care of it." He began to examine one of the graces. "Finding a switch will be our best bet."

Trixie shrugged her shoulders, but she did as she was told. She highly doubted that it would be that easy to get to the Sapphire Rose. As her fingers trailed across the base, she felt a piece of the statue give under her finger. She pressed down harder and faintly heard the clanking of gears.

The quartet took a step back as the statue began to shake. Slowly, it moved to the side, revealing a flight of stairs spiraling downward. Trixie tried to quell the adrenaline rush she had as she traded nervous glances with the others.

"Well," Leo said after a moment, "I guess we go in."

The other three silently nodded. Leo led the way with Trixie and the siblings behind him. When the statue slid back into place behind them, it became pitch black. Trixie quickly called a ball of fire to light the way.

After what felt like ages, the stairwell finally came to a stop. Trixie winced slightly as she stepped into ice-cold ankle-deep water. Pillars lined the area, and she could barely make out old designs etched into the walls. Trixie wrinkled her nose in disgust as she was bombarded with the smell of rotten sardines from all sides.

"Where are we?" Trixie asked, slightly surprised to see her breath.

"I don't know," Leo said as he looked around. "Who would have thought that a place like this existed under the city?"

"These are the catacombs," Starla said as she let her gaze wander around the area. "The under workings of the city. This would be a perfect hiding place for a valuable object since no one would willingly journey down here." She lifted a paw out of the water and shook it daintily.

"Let us hope we do not run into a Minotaur," Orion teased as they slowly ventured into the catacombs.

Trixie jumped as a rat scurried across her foot. "Of all places." Trixie attempted to shake some grime off her shoe. "It has to be in a sewer."

"It could be in a dragon's mouth," Starla said. Trixie turned to glare at her. Starla smiled weakly. "I am not helping, am I?"

Trixie shook her head.

They plunged farther into the catacombs, their ears and eyes trained on their surroundings. Everything seemed to blend together. Trixie was almost sure that there was no end. After a few minutes, they saw a door up ahead. Relieved, they headed in that direction.

A loud splash echoed through the catacombs. The quartet froze as they listened.

"That didn't sound like a rat," Leo whispered as his hand hovered over the hilt of his sword.

Starla sniffed the air. "That does not smell like a rat."

Orion's eyes widened as he noticed a large black mass approaching them. "It certainly does not look like a rat."

As the creature stepped into the light from the ball of fire, Trixie gasped. A half-bull half-man stood before her. "That's because it isn't a rat!"

The Minotaur let out a roar as it charged. They quickly scattered, just barely avoiding his lethal horns. It pawed the ground as it charged Leo. He whipped out his sword and slashed the beast on the chest as he rushed by. The Minotaur let out a howl as it turned and charged at Leo again. Leo blocked his horns and nicked the beast on the shoulder.

As the beast recovered, Leo rolled over toward the others. "It may not be very smart, but it is strong. We need a plan."

"I've got an idea," Trixie pulled out the Harp of Oriantist. "Leo, I need you to distract it so that Orion and Starla can get a grip on it and hold it down. Leave the rest to me."

They nodded as they went to their designated tasks. Leo began to taunt it as he waved the sword around. The Minotaur took the bait and charged at him. Leo dodged just in time. As the beast sailed past, Leo gave it a whack on the back with his sword. Leo repeated this process two more times. Each time, the Minotaur began to slow down.

As the Minotaur prepared to charge once more, Orion and Starla sprang out of the darkness and leapt onto the beast. When they each had a grip on one of the Minotaur's arms, they hurled themselves to the ground, bringing the Minotaur with them.

Knowing she had little time before Starla and Orion lost their grip, Trixie immediately summoned water. The water around them rose and raced toward the Minotaur. Leo, Starla and Orion jumped out of the way just as the Minotaur was slammed by the water. The force sent it flying at the wall. The pressure of the water caused the Minotaur to crash into the wall, unable to move.

Still playing the string for water, Trixie also played the string for ice. Slowly, the water began to freeze. When she stopped playing, the Minotaur was frozen against the wall.

It tried to move; and, when it realized it couldn't, it let out a howl.

With a grin, Trixie placed the harp back in her pack. "That ought to keep it busy for a while."

"Nice move." Leo sheathed his sword.

They gave a fleeting glance toward the Minotaur before proceeding through the door.

Once through the door, Trixie noted how the atmosphere changed dramatically. Instead of the slimy catacombs, they were in what looked like a paved courtyard. Forest green vines had grown wild covering almost every inch of the pillars that lined the room. In the center of the room was the Sapphire Rose.

The single rose sat on top of a bush, its bloom reaching up to the dim light that filtered through the ceiling. It was a deep sapphire color, and its petals looked like velvet. Its thorns, Trixie noticed, were tipped with a blood-red color. In the lighting, it looked as magical and ethereal as the legend said it was.

"I can't believe it," Leo said in astonishment.

"Me neither," Trixie added. "I suppose we need to pick it; don't we?"

"What did the riddle say about the rose again?" Starla asked.

Trixie quickly pulled out Book who repeated the riddle.

In its petals, it holds life
And in its thorns, it holds death.
The paradox lies where the three graces of humanity meet.
There shall it forever remain, protected by its own power
And only will it be removed again by a virgin's touch."

"It says that it can only be removed again by a virgin's touch," Orion said. All eyes turned to Trixie.

"Trixie," Leo said, slightly uncomfortable with what he was about to ask. "You are still a virgin, right?"

"Last time I checked I was." She glanced at the Sapphire Rose and sighed. "Oh, boy."

"Mera," Starla said, "if you are worried, you do not have to do this."

Trixie shook her head. "The riddle said that it can only be picked by a virgin's touch." She sighed again. "I am a virgin so I qualify. I just hope the riddle is right."

Taking a deep breath, Trixie approached the rose. She could feel an electric charge surrounding it. She hesitated slightly before reaching out.

Closing her eyes, she grasped the rose. She opened her eyes, surprised that she hadn't been pricked. She looked down and saw that, although the thorns were pressed against her hand, they did not hurt her. The rose opened into a full bloom and seemed to glow. With a slight pull, the Sapphire Rose broke off with ease. With a grin, she held the rose out to her comrades.

A loud explosion filled the room as chunks of the wall spewed everywhere. Men clad in armor filled the room. Their weapons were trained on all four of them. Something hit Trixie hard in the back of her head. As she fell, a face came into her line of vision. Her eyes widened as recognition set in.

"Mordrid." She weakly clutched the rose to her chest. "You did this."

Her vision slowly faded as he lifted her chin and said, "I knew if I had someone follow you, it would only be a matter of time before you led me to the Sapphire Rose."

His laughter was the last thing she heard as she faded into darkness.

Chapter 19:

CAPTURED

THE first thing Trixie noticed when she regained consciousness was how cold it was. A chill seeped into her bones, and her body ached every time she moved. Also, the dull throbbing in her head was not helping matters. She opened her eyes, and the memories came rushing back to her.

Mordrid had betrayed them. Starla and Leo had been right all along, yet she had been too stubborn to believe it might be true. He had seemed so nice and caring when he helped her. *I guess you really can't judge a book by its cover,* Trixie thought as she rubbed the back of her head.

"I see you are finally awake," Mordrid said as he slowly came into the light. "I hope you like your living quarters." Glancing around, Trixie noticed that she was in a small room. There were no windows and only one steel-plated door that led to the outside. To her dismay, she was chained by her ankles to the wall.

"Yeah, but I would like to complain to the manager. The air conditioner seems to be on the fritz." Trixie crossed her arms and glared.

Mordrid shrugged as he continued. "While you were resting, I took the liberty of taking your bag. You know, you carry around a lot of interesting stuff." He grinned as he pulled out the Harp of Oriantist. "For instance, this harp. It looks harmless enough, but I have witnessed its true potential with its fight against the Minotaur." He placed the harp aside. "As for this…" he pulled out Book and examined it. "I know it has potential."

Book immediately flipped itself open in Mordrid's arms. His eyes widened as he read what Book wrote. A minute later, he became angry and threw it at Trixie. "This is useless. You can keep it." As he scooped the harp up, he walked toward the door. Glancing back, he said, "I'll be back for you later. We have unfinished business concerning the Sapphire Rose."

Once he left, Trixie glanced down at what Book had written. Two whole pages were completely filled with words:

Cochon

Svinja

Prase

Gris

Varken

Sika

Schwein

Maiale

Buta

Porco

Porc

Cerdo

Vark

Pecga

Khzooyrraa

Txerri

Shuor

"What did you say?" Trixie asked.

"Oh, I was just calling him a pig in different languages. As if I would tell him anything interesting."

Trixie sat in silence. Later, as she was about to fall asleep, the door opened with a loud creak. Mordrid stepped inside.

"Rise and shine, sunshine. You're coming with me."

Trixie glared at him as he dragged her to her feet. She was slowly led out of her cell and down a hallway. It only took a second for her to realize that they were in the High Council's building.

"What do the other members of the council think of you kidnapping me?" Trixie asked.

Mordrid laughed. "The High Council are nothing but yes men. They are willing to do anything to appease Dirdrom."

Trixie's eyes widened as she looked at Mordrid. "You know of Dirdrom? Then you must realize that he doesn't care about your world. He only wants to control it and use it for his own means…"

She trailed off as Mordrid began to laugh again. "Honestly, for a smart girl such as yourself, you can be so dense." He leaned closer toward her face. "Write my name backwards and what does it spell?"

Trixie's eyes widened as she realized what he meant.

"So you figured it out then?" he asked. "I am Dirdrom." He took a step back as smoke engulfed him. A moment later, a tall, lanky-built man stood where Mordrid had been. He was pale with no hair and bright red eyes. "This is how I really look," Dirdrom said, his voice much deeper than Mordrid's and a lot more sinister. He snapped his fingers; and, in a blink of an eye, he was back to Mordrid. "But personally, I like this form better." He grabbed her arm and dragged her forward once more.

"Well, personally, I think both forms stink," Trixie said.

Mordrid glared at her, his mouth turned up in a sneer. "Come on; the public awaits."

They went through a door, and Trixie found herself standing on a balcony. Below, all of Crangor City had turned out. Mordrid handed her to a guard and said, "Keep an eye on her." Then he headed over to the microphone on the podium.

He smiled at the audience as he cleared his throat and began his speech. "Citizens of Crangor! As you all know, my father is busy trying to make our world a better place. Because of this, he has asked me to bring to you such joyous news." He paused and let his eyes roam over the crowd. "The Sapphire Rose has been found, and we are in possession of it."

The crowd roared in excitement as they applauded. He held up his hand to quiet them. "We now have the ability to stop the Toracs' attacks. Their crimes are unforgivable, and they must be punished."

The crowd cheered, pleased with Mordrid's words. He held his hand up once more, asking for silence. "They believe what they are doing is right, but we all know that violence is not the answer." He banged his fist on the podium. "With the Sapphire Rose, we will triumph over the evil acts the Toracs are committing; and we shall bring peace to Orcania once more." He threw his fist into the air. "For us! For Orcania!"

The crowd cheered in response, their roars almost deafening. With a smirk plastered on his face, he grabbed Trixie's wrist and dragged her back inside.

"Now that that is done," he murmured, "time to get down to business."

He opened the door, and Trixie found herself in the throne room once more. It had completely changed. Everything was in tattered ruins. The draperies were torn and thrown to the ground, and the throne was overturned. Off to the side was a giant metal machine that resembled a cannon.

"Did a tornado attack while I was gone?" Trixie asked trying to keep her expression neutral.

"Oh, no," Mordrid said, "I just did some remodeling." He pointed to the machine. "My little baby needed a place to stay until it was ready to go."

"What is it for?" Trixie asked, hoping to stall him until she figured out a way to escape.

Mordrid laughed. "I'm glad you asked. This little baby right here is known as the Devastator." Seeing Trixie's amused smirk, he continued, "I know, it is a cliché name; but it is true to its name. It has enough power to wipe out entire armies." He paused as he patted the machine fondly. "I will never have to worry about anyone ever opposing me again."

"If it is as great as you say it is, then why have you never used it?" Trixie asked. She looked to the door and saw two guards standing on each side. She wouldn't be able to escape through there.

Mordrid sighed as a finger trailed across the machine. "That is where you come in. You see, the only way this machine can work is if it has a powerful source of energy running it." He pointed to the broken table on his left. "The Sapphire Rose has the power I need."

Trixie looked more closely at the table. She was surprised to see the rose lying defenseless.

"It seems," Mordrid said, bringing Trixie back to the present, "there is a little predicament on our hands. You see, the Sapphire Rose seems to have taken a liking to you. It only wants you to hold it. I've already lost a few men trying to move it to the Devastator."

Trixie was only slightly surprised to see that Mordrid showed no remorse for those he sacrificed.

"Now," Mordrid said as he looked up at her, "I need you to pick up the rose and place it into the Devastator."

Trixie raised an eyebrow as she laughed. "You don't honestly believe that I am going to do that. I would rather die than help you."

An evil grin flashed across Mordrid's face. "Oh, your life isn't the one on the line." He walked toward her, a grin still plastered on his face. "I know you are one of those noble types who would sacrifice herself to save the others. But," he said as he stopped in front of her, "even noble people have their weaknesses." Before she could react, Mordrid grabbed Book from her hands and held it between his fingers. "For instance," he continued, "I happen to know that you will be willing to do what I say if you knew that the lives of this book, your harp, and your friend, Glade, were in your hands." He shook Book for emphasis. "Even if you have the guts to sacrifice them, there will be others. I will kill all your friends, one by one, until you crack like an egg."

Her glare faltered slightly. He was right. She didn't want her friends to die because she was too stubborn to submit to this arrogant monster. The problem now was whether she was willing to sacrifice three innocent people or risk the lives of others.

It was a difficult decision, but she knew she had to act quickly. If she wanted to live by the belief that the end justifies the means, then she would have to be willing to play executioner, a job she never wished to do.

It all boiled down to one thought, trust. Did she trust Leo and the others enough to willingly play Mordrid's game for now, or should she take matters into her own hands?

She was terrified. Her mind wanted to freeze and tune out what was going on. How was she supposed to make this choice? She was just a kid. She didn't know the answer. How could she risk lives?

She could feel the rose calling out to her, telling her that the choice she made would be the right one.

Trixie sighed as she reached for the rose. "They're going to beat you."

Mordrid laughed. "If you say so."

I'm trusting you, Leo, Trixie thought as she placed the Sapphire Rose inside the machine. Its glowing reminded her of the rhythm of a heartbeat. *Please don't prove me wrong.*

Chapter 20:

THE RESCUE

AFTER the Devastator was up and running, Mordrid took Trixie back to the cell where he unceremoniously threw her inside. As she rubbed her sore rear, he threw Book down beside her and slammed the cell door shut. As her eyes took time to adjust, Trixie realized that she wasn't alone. Although the dim lighting allowed her to see a figure sitting in a shadowed corner, she could barely see the shape.

After a moment, the figure spoke. "Don't I know you?" Her voice sounded weak, but there was still evidence that it generally carried a lilt. When she spoke, Trixie caught a whiff of flowers.

Trixie squinted into the darkness. "Can you step into the light?"

The figure obliged, and Trixie gasped when she recognized the figure. Glade, the spirit of the wood, stood before her, gaunt, with dark circles under her eyes. She looked tired and less spirited.

"I know you," Glade repeated.

Trixie nodded. "We've met. I am..." she paused as she remembered her situation, "was the keeper of the Harp of Oriantist."

Glade's eyes widened with recognition. "I remember now. You were at the trials." Her frown returned. "But why are you here?"

"We were trying to find you. We followed you through the portal and ended up here."

Glade's face lit up with excitement. "You've come to rescue me." Her face became gloomy again. "But, you've been captured as well."

Trixie reached out to Glade. "Don't worry," she said smiling. "Leo and the others are planning to break us out."

Glade looked down at her clasped hands. "As long as Dirdrom doesn't have the Sapphire Rose, there is still hope."

Trixie winced, hating herself for what she was about to say. "I'm afraid the Sapphire Rose is in his possession."

Glade's eyes widened as her hands dropped to her sides.

"But don't worry," Trixie said. "We are going to get it back."

Glade leaned against the wall as her shoulders drooped. "It is hopeless. If he has the rose, there is no hope for us."

Trixie frowned. She was slightly irritated with Glade's depression. "Look, not all is lost. You've just got to believe."

Glade laughed, her eyes darkening. "Believe in what?"

Trixie stood up with her hands on her hips. "Well, for one thing, believe that we are going to be rescued and that we are going to beat Dirdrom. If we act negative, then we're never going to win."

Glade stared at her curiously. "You really believe that, don't you?"

Trixie nodded. "I know it."

A large explosion occurred, as the wall with the door crumpled. Rocks were blown everywhere as Trixie and Glade pressed themselves against the back wall. As the smoke cleared, Trixie looked up to see Leo, Starla and Orion before her.

With a grin, Leo hoisted the Dark Blade over his shoulder. "Did somebody call for a rescue team?"

Trixie grinned as she scooped Book up into her arms. "I was wondering if you would ever come."

Starla ran up to Trixie and gave her a lick across her face. "Mera, I am so glad you are safe."

"Hey," Orion said as he cocked his head, "is that Glade?"

All eyes turned towards Glade, who waved her hand sheepishly.

Reminded of the situation at hand, Trixie turned her attention to Leo. "Guys, we have a problem."

After Trixie recounted the events about the loss of her harp and the whereabouts of the Sapphire Rose, Leo explained how they got there. The Toracs staged an attack to provide a diversion for Leo, Starla and Orion to rescue her.

Leo ran a hand through his hair. "This is bad, but at least the Devastator isn't working yet. He hasn't fired on us, so that means we still have time."

"But there is no way we are going to be able to get it," Trixie pressed her lips into a thin line. "With the attack, Dirdrom will put his top guards around it." She stared down at her hands. "Plus, I don't have my harp, so I won't be any help."

Leo paced back and forth. "Okay, I guess our best bet is to go after your harp first. With it, we can probably overpower the guards and get to the Devastator."

"I overheard one of the guards while we were sneaking around," Starla said. "I do believe they are keeping your harp along with the other confiscated items in a room a couple halls back."

Trixie glanced at Glade. "You feel up to coming with us?"

Glade grinned. "Are you kidding? I can't wait to get out of this horrible place."

The explosions outside alerted Trixie to the fact that the Toracs were doing all they could to give them plenty of time to get out of there. This thought quickened her pace. Starla and Orion led, their noses to the ground, as they slinked through the corridors.

After a couple of turns, they reached the room. The door was locked, and there were no guards in sight.

"This is too easy," Leo said as he looked around.

"Something's wrong," Trixie stared up at the ceiling to see if there were any cameras. "Why would they leave a room full of confiscated items unguarded?"

Everyone traded glances as the question ran through their heads.

"Come on," Orion said after a moment. "We do not have much time."

Snapping out of her stupor, Trixie quickly followed the others inside.

The room was dimly lit. A table ran along a back wall with different items piled on top. In the center of the pile was the Harp of Oriantist.

"Wow," Trixie said, "I am getting major déjà vu."

Leo was about to step forward when Glade's hand shot out. He gave her a questioning look, but Glade merely pointed upward. "There's a sniper plant growing in here."

Trixie saw a strange purple vine-like plant growing on the walls. It's bulbs had pointed teeth, reminding her of a larger version of a Venus Fly Trap. Book quickly flipped open, "*Snipers are carnivorous plants known for shooting darts that cause drowsiness. Once their prey falls asleep, they wrap their vines around their prey and strangle them.*"

"Well, now we know why there are no guards out front," Starla said.

"Do you think you can prevent it from attacking us?" Leo asked Glade.

She shook her head. "I'm afraid I am so weak I cannot connect with the plants of this world." She leaned against the wall for support. "If only we were back in Quarteze."

"Don't worry about it," Trixie said. "We can handle it." She looked at Leo. "Ready, Leo?"

Leo nodded. Taking a deep breath, they ran into the room. As soon as they entered the room, the bulbs opened and tiny thorns sailed at Leo and Trixie. Leo blocked for them using the Dark Blade. Trixie grabbed the Harp of Oriantist. As she reached out, a dart struck her in the wrist. It dissolved a second later. She stared at her wrist dumbfounded.

"Hey," Leo panted, "what are you waiting for?"

Trixie shook her head to clear her thoughts. She clutched the harp as she followed Leo out. As they shut the door to the room, Trixie started to feel dizzy.

Glade frowned as she felt her forehead. "Are you all right?"

"I feel a little dizzy, that's all," Trixie said. Her wrist throbbed, and she saw that it was swollen. She could feel her eyelids drooping.

Leo's eyes widened. "Trixie, you've been hit."

"Oh my," Trixie's eyes rolled up to the top of her head as she collapsed. She felt herself being lifted by someone. Without a second thought, she snuggled into her new pillow.

In the distance, she could hear Leo saying something about needing to leave. There was a flash of light. Then she knew no more.

Chapter 21:

PREPARATION FOR BATTLE

TRIXIE regained consciousness a couple of times after her blackout. They didn't last long, however, since exhaustion would always claim her quickly. Each time, she was forced to drink a foul tasting liquid before slipping into a dreamless sleep.

Finally, after what seemed like ages, Trixie was able to stay awake even though she was still groggy. She noticed that she was no longer in the High Council's building.

"Glad to see you're finally up," Leo said as he emerged from a dark corner.

Trixie yawned and rubbed her eyes. "What happened?"

"You don't remember? The sniper plant attacked you."

Trixie nodded as the memories came back to her. "Yeah, now I remember." She touched her wrist gingerly. "Right before I passed out, I remember seeing a flash of white light. What was that?"

"Dirdrom was able to get the Devastator running." Leo knelt in front of her. "The Toracs took a major blow."

Trixie slowly shook her head. "This is all my fault," she whispered. "If I hadn't helped him…"

"It's not your fault," Leo said as he placed a hand on hers. "Our job was to save Glade, and that's what we did. You aren't expected to save the world."

Trixie looked into Leo's eyes. "You know we are already in too deep. We can't just walk away now. Not with all that we know."

Leo nodded and let his focus drift to the open tent flap. "Yeah, I know." He grinned slightly. "I guess we might as well see what the Toracs have decided to do." He offered Trixie his hand. She stood up, her legs wobbling slightly. After a moment, they were steady; and she followed Leo outside.

She was surprised to see the Toracs were packing their belongings. Their faces were sullen as they loaded cowtows with their supplies. Starla and Orion were frantically running around trying to convince them not to leave.

"What is going on?" Trixie asked.

Jamul heard her and walked over. "We're leaving. After what happened, there's no point staying here."

"You're giving up?" Leo asked. Orion and Starla walked over, the fur on the back of their necks raised.

"We tried to stop them," Starla said.

"But they just will not listen," Orion added.

Frustration built up within Trixie. "Hey!" she yelled. No one paid attention. She glanced at Orion and Starla. They got the message. Orion let out a loud roar while Starla howled.

Everyone stopped in their tracks and turned their attention to Trixie.

"I can't believe you," Trixie said, her fists clenched. "You are just giving up?"

"What's the point?" a Torac yelled. "We'll just get killed."

"So, you are going to let those who died in the last attack die in vain?" Leo asked. "You're not going to even try?"

The Toracs remained silent.

"This is ridiculous," Trixie said, her hands on her hips. "I thought you were the Toracs, determined to win this war. Not wimps." She glanced at Jamul. "Yes, you suffered a loss. In war, you will have loss; but that doesn't mean you should give up." She turned her attention back to the Toracs. "This is your home, your way of life, that you are fighting for. If you don't fight, then who will? Are you going to let Dirdrom destroy what Orcania really is without putting up a fight?"

Some of the Toracs resumed their packing. One growl from Orion and Starla, however, stopped them in their tracks.

"Leo, Starla, Orion and I may not be from your world; but we're not ready to give up. Dirdrom is not going to stop here. He will take over each world one by one until he controls all of them." She pounded her fist into her hand. "I don't want that to happen, and I don't think any of you want that to happen either."

"But we don't have the spirits on our side," another Torac said. "How are we going to beat the Devastator?"

"You're all great people," Trixie said. "I've seen what you can do; and I know we can do it. So, spirits or not, let's show them what we're made of and kick their butts."

There was a collective gasp as Trixie felt something land behind her. Looking back, she came face to face with Aktoe. Craning her neck, she could see all the spirits were outlining the camp. Plue came up next to Trixie and rubbed against her cheek.

Aktoe cocked his head. "How about we make things easier for you. The Council of Ten voted to help you fight Dirdrom." He grinned at Trixie. "After all, we want to protect Orcania."

Trixie could feel the excitement rushing through the crowd. With the spirits on their side, anything was possible. Turning back to the crowd, she said, "So how about it? Let's do it for Orcania!"

A loud roar emitted from the crowd, and Trixie knew they were ready to fight.

"You sure know how to stir up a crowd," Leo whispered.

Trixie just grinned.

It was decided that Jamul, a few of his officers and a couple of spirits were to lay out the plans. The plan was for Jamul and his army to take care of Dirdrom's army while Trixie, Starla, Leo and Orion went after Dirdrom and the Devastator. Since Trixie had seen the Devastator, they believed that she was the most qualified to disable the machine.

Afraid that she was still suffering from the side effects of the sniper plant, Trixie was forced to go to bed once more. She was angry about being forced to bed, but she fell asleep as soon as her head hit the pillow.

Trixie opened her eyes and found herself inside a dark room. A single light from the ceiling shone down on her. She was sitting in a chair and facing the young girl she had seen before.

The girl giggled as she leaned back in her chair. "Hey!"

Trixie crossed her arms. "Who are you and why do you keep appearing in my dreams?"

The girl's legs swung back and forth. "I am me."

Trixie cocked. "What?"

The girl sighed. "I am me."

Trixie awoke with a start. Gasping for air, she looked around and saw Glade sitting in a corner watching her.

"Bad dreams?" Glade asked.

Trixie sighed. "I've been seeing this girl in my dreams. A couple of times, I think I saw her when I was awake as well. She wears a hooded cape, so I can't see her face. I feel like I know her but..."

"I do not know what to tell you," Glade said. "Generally, when you see a spirit of some sort in your dreams and in real life, it means that the spirit is evil; and it wants something from you." She shook her head. "But in your case, that does not sound quite right. She has not harmed you, has she?"

Trixie shook her head. "On the contrary, she's helped me."

Glade frowned. "Well, there is another reason why..." She shook her head again. "Never mind, I see no reason for you to worry over something as trivial as what I'm thinking. You are fine for now, so there is no need to worry."

Leo entered the tent, his expression serious. "It's been decided. We're attacking at dawn."

That night, Trixie couldn't sleep. She tossed and turned, but her mind wouldn't leave the fact that they were going to war the next day. Glancing at Starla and Orion, she saw that they were fast asleep.

How can they rest so easily? she thought as she sat up.

"Can't sleep either?" Leo asked as he sat up as well.

Trixie shook her head. "Too nervous. After all, we're going to war tomorrow."

"Yeah," Leo said with a sigh.

Before she could stop herself, the words tumbled out of her mouth. "Leo, please don't die tomorrow."

Leo's lips twitched. "Where did that come from?"

Trixie turned away, a blush crept up her cheeks. "Just don't die. I would be really upset."

"Okay," Leo said. "I'll try." He hesitated for a moment before asking, "You didn't...like *like* Mordrid did you?"

Trixie shook her head. "No, why?"

"Nothing," Leo laid down. "Just asking."

Starla and Orion snickered. Trixie and Leo looked over at them, but they continued to fake sleeping.

"I guess we should probably try to get some sleep," Trixie said as she lay her head down.

"Yeah," Leo rolled away from her. "Goodnight."

"Night." Trixie said.

As dawn crept over the horizon, the Toracs gathered. A sense of excitement rushed through them. This was it for them. They were about to begin the fight of their lives.

Chapter 22:

THE WAR OF THE ROSE

S ILENTLY, the Toracs left their campsite. They held whatever weapons
they could find which included swords, knifes, old guns, bows and
arrows, shovels and pitchforks. Glade stayed with the women and
children, because she was still weak from her ordeal. Plus, Trixie and
Leo didn't want to lose her again after what they went through to find
her. Some Toracs went out in kadirs while others walked. The spirits
followed close behind.

Trixie, Leo, Starla, Orion, and Jamul stood on one kadir, leading the
way. As they approached the top of a hill, they were able to see Crangor
City below.

A large army stood outside the gate. They were carrying all sorts of
guns and swords. Standing on top of the gate were archers.

"It seems that we are expected," Jamul said as he surveyed the scene.
He glanced back at the small army that was assembled behind them
before he turned to Trixie and Leo. "Well, you ready?"

They nodded. "Let's do this," Trixie said.

Jamul raised his fist into the air. "For Orcania!"

The call was echoed as the Toracs poured over the hill.

In response, archers sent their arrows sailing through the air. From
out of nowhere, Aktoe appeared. Letting out a loud cry, he flapped
his wings once, sending the arrows flying away from the Toracs. They
landed in a row to the side.

The archers, surprised by Aktoe's appearance, fumbled with their
arrows as their commander shouted orders.

As the Toracs continued their charge, the archers sent another volley of arrows their way. Infernia quickly set them on fire while Aktoe sent the remains flying in another direction.

Aktoe and Terra looked at each other before combining their powers, sending a sandstorm flying in the army's direction. With the army momentarily blinded, the Toracs attacked the soldiers guarding the gates.

"Go," Jamul said as he sliced at one of the enemies. "We'll cover you."

The quartet split from the group and headed into the city. Trixie felt raindrops fall from overhead. She looked up and saw Aquaritus riding a huge water ball.

"Look at me," he yelled as he did a handstand. "I brought da water to da desert." He sent the water hurling at nearby troops.

The archers screamed as they jumped from their posts. Their bows had turned into trees while lightning struck at them.

When they reached the High Council's office, it had already suffered some damage from the attack. Dodging a few of Dirdrom's troops, they quickly entered the building.

Because of the building's elevation, Trixie was able to catch a glimpse of the battlefield.

She laughed when she noticed what Aktoe had done with the first volley of arrows. He had them form the word boo in the sand. *No wonder the guards had been startled*, Trixie thought.

"Come on." Orion yelled.

They quickly took the elevator. They were about to press the button to the area they needed to go when the elevator started moving on its own.

"This can't be good," Leo said as they watched the light flash at each floor. It stopped abruptly; and the doors opened, revealing two monsters staring at them. Each had a snake's head, bird's beak, the body of a lion, and their two back legs were bird's feet. Their forked tongues flicked out as they watched the quartet hungrily.

"What are those things?" Trixie asked.

"Don't know, don't care." Leo brandished his sword. "They're in our way."

With a hiss, the creatures attacked. One attacked Starla and Orion while the other went for Trixie and Leo. Leo slashed his sword at the creature, but it dodged every time.

Taking a deep breath, Trixie played the strings to summon an elemental beast. She hoped that even though it had been awhile, she was still able to do it. To her relief, the spell worked, as a giant dragon made out of water raced toward the creature. With a beat of its wings, the dragon sent the creature into the wall behind it.

"Whoa!" Orion said as he stared at the water dragon. "I did not know you could do that."

"Pay attention," Starla said as she blocked an attack directed at Orion.

Orion shook his head and turned back to the creature he was fighting.

The other creature let out a hiss and attacked Leo and Trixie once more. Leo barely dodged it, quickly spinning around and hitting the creature on the back. It tumbled forward, giving Trixie the chance to let her dragon attack again. With one swoop, the dragon was upon it. The creature twisted and turned a couple of times before going limp and fading away.

Starla and Orion were struggling with the other creature. They were rolling around hissing, slashing, and biting, making it difficult for Trixie to distinguish between them. Venom shot out in her direction. Leo pushed her out of the way just in time. The venom hit the wall behind them with a sickening splat. There was a hissing sound as the venom ate away at the wall.

"Ew," Trixie said with a grimace.

"I'm glad that didn't hit us," Leo added.

Orion and Starla seemed to have had enough. They both charged together at the creature and sent it flying into the wall. It hit with a loud cracking sound and slowly faded away.

"What were those things?" Leo asked.

"I do not know," Starla panted. "But they seemed to be some sort of fiend."

Trixie's pack began to rattle. Since there was no one around, she felt it was safe to bring Book out. She quickly pulled it out as she caught her breath.

"Do you know what you just fought? Those were Rainshay. A dangerous form of fiend. Unlike most fiends in Orcania, they do not need to be attached to someone in order to exist. They are known for carrying the mad gene, which accounts for their tendency to have violent outbursts. In other words, they are not a family friendly pet."

"Look out!" Leo yelled as he pointed to something behind her.

Whirling around, Trixie came face to face with Roger, one of the men who had saved her when she first arrived in Orcania. He had his sword raised over his head. Just as he brought it down, Calloway appeared and blocked the sword. He quickly disarmed Roger and slashed his sword at him. Roger took a step back, let out a roar, and faded away.

Everyone stood in stunned silence.

"He was a fiend?" Leo said.

"Well, I'll be," Calloway said as he put away his sword. "I knew there was something off about that fellow."

"It seems Dirdrom did not mind breaking this world's rules," Starla said.

Orion stared warily at the spot where Roger disappeared. He acted as if he was afraid Roger would reappear again.

"Who's he?" Leo pointed to Calloway.

Trixie grinned as she turned to the rest of the group. "Everyone, meet Calloway. One of the men who saved me when I first arrived here."

"Well, then you should know that under the circumstances, we cannot be trusting," Starla said.

"Starla..." Trixie began.

He shook his head. "Say no more. I already know about Dirdrom. In fact, I've been undercover for some time trying to figure out what he's been planning." He ran his fingers through his hair. "I guess I just didn't figure it out quick enough."

"Do you know where he is at the moment?" Leo asked.

Calloway raised an eyebrow. "Don't tell me you four are planning to take on Dirdrom by yourselves."

"That is the general idea," Orion said.

"You can't be serious," Calloway said.

"Let's just say we've had practice saving the world," Trixie said.

Calloway looked at each of them. When he realized they were serious, he let out sigh. "Well, if your minds are made up, I'll show you where he is." He glanced at the elevator. It was completely wrecked. "Looks like we're taking the long way."

They quickly followed him through the corridors. As they rounded a corner, a huge flash lit up the area as the earth quaked. Everyone froze.

"Oh no," Leo said, his face pale. "He's using the Devastator again."

This hastened their pace. The Devastator fired two more times causing Trixie to wonder if there would be anything left to save. After what felt like ages, they finally reached the double doors of the throne room.

"He's through there," Calloway said, pointing to the doors.

"Thank you so much," Trixie said.

"Do you mind helping the Toracs while we take care of him?" Leo asked.

"No problem." Calloway saluted them. He quickly turned the corner and was gone.

Taking a collective deep breath, the quartet turned back toward the double doors.

"You ready?" Leo asked.

Trixie nodded. "Let's do this."

Without hesitation, they opened the doors.

Chapter 23:

THE END OR MERELY THE BEGINNING?

THE throne room was just as she had seen it before. There was wreckage everywhere. The Devastator sat where she had originally seen it. Humming slightly, it was powering up for another attack. The only thing missing from this scene was Dirdrom. He was nowhere in sight.

"I thought Calloway said he was in here," Leo muttered as he held his sword in front of them.

"I don't know." Trixie unconsciously fiddled with the harp. "Something's not right."

Starla and Orion began to growl. Their eyes were glowing as the hair on their backs rose up.

"What is it?" Trixie asked.

They continued to growl.

All of the sudden, a strange taste filled her mouth. It was foul, like a combination of rotten eggs and spoiled milk. No matter what she did, she couldn't get rid of it. She bent over as she dry heaved. Glancing over at Leo, she noticed he was doing the same thing.

"It's rather curious, isn't it?" Dirdrom said as he appeared in front of them. "The deeper you delve into the world of magic, the more in tune you are when something changes." He was in his original form, but a strange black haze surrounded him. Although it was a haze, it seemed to ooze like slime across his body.

As he took a step closer, the foul taste worsened as Leo and Trixie began to dry heave once more.

"Chaos," Starla growled, as the hair on her back stood up even higher.

"To think this power was here all this time, and all I had to do was bend a few rules in this world," Dirdrom clasped his hands behind his back.

Trixie's eyes watered as she went down to one knee. She could sense her fellow companions struggling to stay up as well. The black ooze seemed to thicken on Dirdrom's body. His eyes had turned blood red; and, when he opened his mouth, all she could see was black.

"What's the matter?" Dirdrom asked, his voice sounding almost robotic. "Cat got your tongue?"

"What's going on?" Leo panted. "I can barely keep my sword up."

"That...power..." Orion grunted, "distorting...flow..."

"Why don't you just give up," Dirdrom said as he circled around the quartet. "You're no match for me. You're just kids." He paused, and an evil grin appeared on his face. "Didn't your mothers ever tell you not to play with weapons?"

Trixie felt herself weakening. She knew she couldn't last much longer. Glancing over at the Devastator, she saw it was about ready to fire again. There was no time. They had no time.

"*Don't give up.*"

Trixie's eyes widened. She recognized that voice. It belonged to the little girl.

"*Don't give up.*" the girl repeated. "*I know you can do it.*"

And she felt she could do it. The strange feeling seemed to evaporate from her. Glancing down, she saw that the Harp of Oriantist was glowing.

Dirdrom's eyes widened. "What are you doing?"

Quickly, she plucked the string for lightning and sent a bolt hurling towards the Devastator. The machine groaned in protest as it shut itself down.

"What have you done?" Dirdrom yelled as he stared at the now destroyed Devastator.

This distraction somehow lifted the spell off the others. They quickly ran to Trixie's side as they readied themselves for what was about to come.

When Dirdrom turned back to them, his eyes were pitch black. "You will pay for what you've done."

He sent a black energy ball hurling toward them. They quickly scattered. Bent down on one knee, Leo pointed the sword at Dirdrom. "Shalazar Tendaray."

Black tentacles leapt from his blade and wrapped around Dirdrom.

Dirdom let out an inhuman howl as he struggled against his binds.

"Trixie," Leo yelled.

Trixie quickly summoned the elemental beast for wood. Vines and branches shot from the ground and came together to form a giant snake. With a hiss, the snake pounced on Dirdrom, covering his entire body with vines and branches, slowly squeezing him.

With another howl, a black light peaked through the gaps in the vines and branches. There was a flash; and Dirdrom was free once more, sending fragments of branches and vines everywhere and destroying Trixie's spell. As the fragments fell, they withered up and died.

Dirdrom grinned as he disappeared.

"Where did he go?" Orion whirled around searching for him.

Leo's eyes widened as he saw something materializing behind Starla. "Starla, behind you."

Starla jumped just as Dirdrom's sword slashed the air where she had been standing.

With a growl, he dematerialized the sword and sent dark energy balls at the quartet. Leo and Orion dodged them in time, but Trixie and Starla caught the full blow.

They were sent flying across the room where Trixie hit the wall with such force that she felt her head rattle.

Starla lay sprawled out on the floor a few feet away from her, disoriented.

Glancing back at Dirdrom, she saw Orion lunge for him. He bit into Dirdrom's shoulder and dug his claws into his sides. Dirdrom let out another inhuman howl as he hurled Orion away from him.

Orion bounced and skidded a couple of feet before coming to a stop. As he stood up, he swayed back and forth.

Leo came up from behind and grabbed Dirdrom's arms. Holding them behind Dirdrom's back, Leo yelled, "Trixie, now!"

Trixie plucked the string for lightning and sent a bolt of lightning hurling towards Dirdrom. He quickly freed himself of Leo and pushed him to the side. He opened his mouth and swallowed the lightning.

"And I thought I could eat anything," Orion muttered as he limped towards Trixie.

Starla pounced on Dirdrom, digging her claws and biting at his exposed flesh.

"Insolent dog!" Dirdrom howled as he zapped her with a ball of energy. Starla fell to the ground, and Dirdrom kicked her to the side.

"Next?" he asked as he turned his attention back to the others.

Trixie sent a ball of fire toward him while Leo sent a wave of dark energy from his sword.

"Teaming up are we?" Dirdrom said. "This should be good." He deflected the dark energy and ate the ball of fire. With a laugh, he added, "I can do this all day."

Trixie, in desperation, looked around the room and caught a glimpse of the Sapphire Rose lying within the Devastator.

Her eyes widened as a thought occurred to her.

"Got a plan?" Orion asked.

Trixie nodded. "Yeah, keep him busy for me."

Orion saluted her. "Roger."

He, along with Starla and Leo, charged at Dirdrom.

Closing her eyes, Trixie concentrated on the Sapphire Rose. Playing the string for plants, she willed the rose to grow.

Opening her eyes, she saw that a vine with red tipped thorns was slowly growing out of the Devastator. Still playing, she made eye contact with Leo. She motioned with her head towards the Devastator.

Seeing the vine, Leo nodded and swung harder at Dirdrom, forcing him toward it. When he was within range, Trixie plucked the string a final time, sending her energy toward the vine. It shot out and wrapped itself around Dirdrom's leg, the thorns biting into the skin, drawing blood.

Dirdrom smirked. "Do you honestly think you can defeat me with a measly vine?"

"You should take a closer look," Trixie said. "That is no ordinary vine."

His eyes followed the vine back to the Devastator. His face paled as he realized what happened. "No!"

His body stiffened as he slowly turned gray. His eyes rolled upward; and he fell backwards, landing with a loud thud.

Starla, Leo and Orion slowly backed away.

A black vortex appeared behind Dirdrom. Black tendrils from the vortex wrapped themselves around him and quickly pulled him back in. Within seconds, the vortex vanished.

"We did it," Leo said as he bent over to catch his breath. "It's over."

"Over for us," Starla said, "but for him, it is only the beginning."

Trixie and Leo frowned.

"What do you mean, only the beginning?" Trixie tightened her grip on the harp.

Orion shrugged casually. "You never mess with that magic. You will always regret it in the end." He added in a hushed voice. "Very painful."

Trixie watched as the vine retreated back into the Devastator. The machine started making a loud beeping noise.

Starla and Orion winced at the high-pitched sound, while Leo and Trixie went over to examine the machine.

Leo's eyes widened. "It's about to self destruct. We need to get the rose out of there."

Squinting, Trixie reached through a crevice for the Sapphire Rose. She could feel the heat coming from the machine. When she had the rose in her grasp, she pulled it out. "We need to get out of here."

"There's no time." Leo said.

"Mera," Starla said, as Orion and she bounded towards them. "Remember what happened with Aquaritus."

Trixie's eyes widened as she remembered the air bubble she had created. "Get close to me." Once they were near, she struck the water and air strings. The bubble encased them, just as the machine exploded.

Much to her relief, the bubble protected them from blowing away, as fire and fragments of the building flew around them.

After the smoke cleared, they were greeted with the ruins of the throne room.

"Hey," Orion said as he shifted from one foot to the other. "Can you release the bubble?" He winced as a drop of water landed on his ear.

Starla butted him playfully. "Scaredy Cat."

Orion glared at her. "Toilet drinker."

Trixie quickly dematerialized the bubble.

Starla puffed up her chest. "How dare you say that. I am a wolf. We do not drink from bowls. We drink from streams."

Orion rolled his eyes. "Blah, blah, blah."

As they continued to bicker, Leo and Trixie traded glances. They were exhausted and achy. The last thing they needed was an argument from the feuding siblings.

"Hey, Orion, Starla?" Trixie said.

They both looked at her.

"Can it!" Leo and Trixie said in unison.

Starla and Orion looked stunned.

"Wonder what is eating them," Orion muttered to Starla.

She just shook her head.

Looking around, Trixie realized that they were standing in the middle of the remains of the High Council building. It had been destroyed in the blast. She had a clear view of Crangor City, and she noticed a large crowd had gathered at the entrance. Faintly, she heard the sounds of cheering.

Starla's ears perked up as she cocked her head. "It sounds like someone is celebrating without us."

"Well, come on," Orion said as he began to pick his way through the rubble. "We cannot allow them to party without us."

They slowly made their way to the fanfare. As they moved closer to the crowd, they saw the Toracs and Dirdrom's army laughing and cheering as they hugged each other.

Leo stopped and stared. "What is going on?"

Jamul spotted them and waved. He quickly made his way over to them. "It was amazing." He hugged each of the quartet's necks. "As soon as the building was destroyed, they surrendered. It turned out they didn't want to fight us in the first place."

Trixie grinned. "Imagine that."

"What happened to the spirits?" Orion asked as he craned his neck.

"Gone," Jamul said, "They left as soon as the battle was over."

Just like spirits, Trixie thought.

Calypso grinned as she walked over to them. "Can you believe it? It's over. We're free." She looked at the crowd and raised her fist. "Long live Orcania!"

"Long live Orcania!" the crowd echoed.

"Looks like you have your work cut out for you," Starla said.

Jamul shrugged, "Yeah, we'll have to repair the damage Crangor City sustained." He winced as he looked at the remains of the High Council building. "And somehow, we have to figure out how to rebuild the High Council building."

"I'm not worried in the least," Trixie said with a grin. "Everything will be fine in your hands."

Jamul blushed as he rubbed the back of his neck.

Calypso placed a loving hand on his shoulder.

Glade drifted away from the crowd and quickly approached them. Her complexion looked better, and she seemed to have a slight glow surrounding her.

"Congratulations," she said. "You did it." She frowned as she looked at the Sapphire Rose in Trixie's hand. "What's wrong with the rose?"

They all gasped as they looked at the rose. It was glowing bright blue. A hush fell over the crowd as the rose left her hand and began to float in the air. There was a flash, and the rose transformed into a light-blue gem.

It floated down and landed in Trixie's hands. It felt smooth and warm. She could see a faint glow from its center. "What the?"

"It has transformed into its true form," a voice said.

Looking up, Trixie saw three young women standing before them. The one on the left wore a simple white dress. It was sleeveless and extended to her mid-thigh. She had long white hair that reached her lower back, and her eyes were milky white. The one on the right looked like her twin except her dress, hair, and eyes were black. The one in the center looked similar except her dress, hair, and eyes were gray.

"Are...you..." Leo asked.

All three grinned as they took their poses.

Trixie's eyes widened. "You're the Three Graces."

They dropped their poses. "You are correct," the one in white said. "I am Charity."

"I am Compassion," the one in black added.

"And I am Hope," said the one in gray.

"We are the protectors of this world's gem," Charity said.

"We were to watch over it until you came," Compassion added

"And then tell you what is about to come," Hope finished.

"Wait a minute," Leo said as he held his hands up. "I'm confused. You said the rose turned back into its original form. Is something about to happen?"

"Something already has happened," Charity said.

"It has started," Starla whispered.

Trixie looked at her curiously, but she said nothing.

"There are eight worlds, including this one, that you must visit," Compassion said. "In each world, you must collect its gem."

"The gem contains the life essence of that world," Hope added as she touched her chest. "It is almost like a heart."

"With them, you can unlock the gateway to the Forgotten World and destroy it," Charity said.

"Destroy what?" Trixie asked.

"The chaos," all three said.

She could hear Starla and Orion growl in the background.

"It is currently trapped inside the Forgotten World, but the seal is slowly breaking," Compassion said.

"You have already seen the effects of it when you fought Dirdrom," Hope said. "That is just a mere sample of its power."

"If it breaks free, then all the worlds are doomed," Charity finished.

"But how do we get there?" Leo asked.

"The worlds have realigned themselves allowing people to cross from one to the other. We can transport you to one of the worlds," Compassion said.

"In each world, there will be someone known as a world hopper who can transport you to another," Hope finished.

"Well," Leo said as he glanced back at the others. "I'm game, but what about you guys?" He held out his hand.

"Of course, I am going," Starla said as she placed her paw on top of his.

"Me, too," Orion said as he placed his paw on top of hers. Seeing Starla's glare he added, "You do not honestly believe I am going to miss out on this?"

"I'm in as well," Trixie said as she placed her hand on top. She glanced back at Glade. "But what are we going to do about Glade?"

"You do not have to worry," Charity said. "After we transport you, we will send Glade back to her world."

The quartet looked at the people surrounding them. The Toracs' eyes were filled with tears, and Dirdrom's army bowed their heads respectfully.

"Well," Trixie said. "I guess this is goodbye."

"Thank you for everything," Jamul said as he hugged each of them. "We will never forget you."

"We'll miss you," Calypso added as she hugged them as well.

"See you around, Glade," Leo said as she hugged him.

Glade turned her attention to Trixie. With a smile, she hugged her. "Thank you," she whispered.

"Are you ready?" Compassion asked.

The quartet nodded.

With the quartet in the center, the Three Graces raised their arms as they pressed their palms against each other forming a triangle. They closed their eyes as their heads looked skyward.

Chanting filled the quartet's ears as each grace glowed their respected color. As the world began to fade away, Trixie couldn't help but grin.

Squeezing Leo's hand, she said, "Here we go again!"

ORCANIA GLOSSARY

Aktoe: Spirit of Wind. He was born when the north, south, west, and east winds met together in a rare occurrence. Ever curious of the goings on in the world, he sends his breezes out to catch snippets of conversations. His knowledge almost rivals that of Shal Ron Lee.

Aquaritus: Spirit of Water. Of all the spirits, Aquaritus is considered the most fun-loving and laid-back of the spirits. His trust in humans has often gotten him in trouble with the Council of Ten. However, like his element, his temper is not something to test. He is known for sinking an entire city because the citizens threw garbage in a nearby ocean.

Arachlophil: Also known as the grass spider, this creature resides deep within forests. Their bodies camouflage perfectly with their surroundings, allowing them to catch their prey with ease. Unfortunately, there are not many left in Orcania due to the loss of their habitats.

Babosa: The babosas are capybara-like creatures that reside in the grasslands. Their main sources of food are insects and vegetation. They were once believed to be a docile form of fiend because of their strange feeler-like appendages. However, this was disproved by the scholar Alphonso Darroway. Although the babosas have a sharp sense of smell, eyesight, and hearing, they prefer to use their feelers to test their surroundings. This has led scholars such as Alphonso to believe that the feelers provide some sort of sixth sense.

Baku Tree: This ancient tree resides within Gardenia's forest. It is believed that the tree was planted by Gardenia when Orcania was first created. It is thousands of years old and seems to be very knowledgeable of worldly matters.

Council of Ten: The Council of Ten is the reigning body of the Spirits. The ten most powerful Spirits gather each year at an appointed location to discuss the matters concerning the Spirits and Orcania. Since there are new spirits appearing all the time, the Council of Ten's body is not set in stone.

Cowtow: A beast known for being similar to a packhorse, and mainly used by merchants and travelers to carry goods. It was originally bred for that purpose so it has many adaptable features that prove necessary for the traveler. The belief that the left eye is magical has never been proven false since all are too scared to see if it is true. One of the old books claims that the eye is supposedly an ice-blue color. This tale also includes a foolhardy boy who decided to break the taboo and gaze upon the eye. Apparently, as soon as he lifted the cowtow's bangs, he died.

Crangor City: Considered the capital of Orcania. All the new inventions are created from the city, and the brightest scholars reside there. It is considered a melting pot because of the many different people who live there. People come from all around in hopes of making money in the city. Because of its diversity, it seems to be separated in two parts: the business/futuristic version and the old traditional version. Orcanians are actually proud of what their city has become because to them it represents two halves working together for a greater goal.

Dark Blade: A weapon from Quarteze originally used by the Warrior of Darkness during the battle of the Shadow One in the Age of Twilight. After the war, the blade disguised itself as two blades so it wouldn't be destroyed like the rest of the weapons of darkness. It is now in its original form once more and resides with its new owner.

Dirdrom: A mysterious and powerful sorcerer. He is rumored to have the ability to create temporary portals to other worlds. This power is supposedly only found within the *Sharonan*, a sage's book that resides in the legendary Library of Quarteze. This is highly unlikely, since scholars do not know the current whereabouts of the library.

Electra: Spirit of Lightning. Although Electra often puts up a tough front, she really is sweet. She is considered the founder of electricity because she allowed her lightning to be harnessed.

Gardenia: Spirit of the Plants. Even from an early age, Gardenia has been extremely paranoid. This is probably because Shal Ron Lee mistook her once for an ordinary rabbit and tried to eat her. Because of her paranoia, it is said that her home is considered an impregnable fortress. No one has ever has ever seen it so we do not know if it is true.

Glade: Spirit of Plants in Quarteze. Glade is often associated with the Spirit of Medicine, Florentine. This is mainly because most remedies are derived from plants. She is known as one of the gentler spirits and rarely provoked to anger. However, when provoked, she can be very deadly. An example of her anger is the Thyme Forest. A village originally lived where Thyme Forest originates. Their main export was thyme. Scholars are unsure what the villagers did to vex Glade, but one day a forest sprouted where the village was. When the villagers returned to their homes, they found that they could no longer grow thyme. To this day, thyme cannot be grown in this area, a reminder of how powerful Glade is.

Glarkeyal: An alligator-like creature found in Orcania. They are generally docile around humans. They eat pest fish and crustaceans so farmers like to keep them around. They spend most of their lives in water and are, in fact, born within the water.

Harp of Oriantist: An ancient weapon of light that was used by the Warrior of Light during the battle with the Shadow One in the Age of Twilight. The weapon is known for its beautiful song, which summons the elements of the world. It is said that its song could stop an ogre in its tracks to stare in awe. The harp currently resides with its new owner.

High Council: The High Council is the reigning governing body of Orcania. It is composed of one delegate from each region of Orcania. This is so that each region has a say over what is going on in Orcania. Since each region has its own needs, this system has proven very effective.

Icia: Spirit of Ice. Unlike her element, Icia is not cold and emotionless. She has always tried to remain kind to the weary traveler; and, because of her kindness, there have not been many deaths from frostbite in Orcania.

Infernia: Spirit of Fire. Infernia resides in the molten lava under the ground. She tends to be a little hot-headed. When she gets angry, she sends massive heat waves through Orcania. She once made lava erupt in the middle of a village.

Kadir: A raft-like mode of transportation to assist travelers through the deserts of Orcania. The kadirs' ability to glide over the sand cuts time for travelers and allows them to avoid many of the deadly creatures of the deserts. It was first invented by Genevieve Doddle. When he traveled the desert on foot, he mistook a mirage of the desert as a river. When he reached a village, he created the kadir to sail that river. Orcanians have used the kadirs ever since.

Lalavines: Spirits who take forms by using the vines around them. No one is quite sure why they choose vines as their bodies. Some believe it is a way to show loyalty and appreciation for Gardenia.

Lullaby Bloom: A special plant found in the open grasslands. When the flowers are absorbing sunlight, they sing. No one is quite sure what it is about their melody that makes people fall asleep. Some scholars have tried to figure it out but have had trouble since they keep falling asleep. If the bloom is mashed and made into a tea, it can be used to cure insomnia.

Macoys: Spirits who take form by using the leaves around them. Scholars are unsure why the spirits choose leaves to take their form. Like the lalavines, they believe the macoys are showing appreciation and loyalty to Gardenia.

Miniature Dolphins: Created when the need for small water transportation was required in Crangor City. Miniature Dolphins share many characteristics with their cousins, the regular dolphins, except they cannot stay underwater as long. No one is sure why the miniature dolphins lost that trait. Some hypothesize it is because of all the inbreeding.

Minotaur: Unlike common belief, Minotaurs do not reside only in mazes. They will reside anywhere that is dark and moist. Their favorite meal is rat since they are common among their homes. They also have a taste for bats. Like the bats, they have very poor eyesight. It is said that if a Minotaur were to ever be exposed to the sun, it would go blind and slowly deteriorate. Of course, this theory has never been proven.

Night Mares: A double entendre, night mares are mostly mares that are nocturnal and give people, who look into their eyes, nightmares. No one is sure why the stallions choose to live solitary lives. Some believe it is because of the night mares' structural class order that prevents them from joining groups. In ancient texts, it is stated that night mares have psychic abilities, which is why they can give anyone nightmares if one looks into their eyes. Night mares develop this ability after a few weeks of age. Sadly, because of their tendency to give people nightmares, they are often treated as pests. The truth is that night mares would rather be left alone than engage in a fight.

Null Void Zone: An area in Orcania where no magic can exist. Because of the strong magnetic field, magic is somehow blocked. This has made many scholars ponder why magnetism prevents magic. Ancient sages stated that magic is a delicate balance of power that can be affected easily. They believe that the magnetism of the null void pulls and pushes it around so much that it is already destroyed by the time it reaches the user. This has led people to wonder where magic really does come from.

Oracle Tree: Also known as the clear-sighted tree. It is said that if one were to eat the juices of the oracle tree's fruit, it will promote clarity and a higher sense of being. The Shinobi tribes use the juices from its fruits in most of their ceremonies.

Ore: Spirit of Metal. Unlike his brethren spirits, he is more solemn and quiet. He spends most of his time in the bowels of the earth creating new weapons out of metal. Supposedly, he made a deal with Infernia so that he could have the hottest fires to make his powerful weapons. If someone were to receive one of his weapons, it is said that he or she would be invincible.

People of the Desert: A tribe that lives in the desert regions of Orcania. The People of the Desert are a rather kind bunch who value water over gold. Their original ancestors were nomads who wandered the edges of the desert in search of life. They know every aspect of the desert and could navigate it with their eyes closed. If one is ever in trouble in the desert, it is always best to find one of these people.

People of the Forest: A tribe that lives in the forests of Orcania. The People of the Forest are often mistaken as gypsies because of their style of clothing and their tendency of never settling down in one place. All their foods, clothing, and supplies are made naturally to respect the forests. They are knowledgeable of herbal remedies.

People of the Mountains: A tribe that lives in the mountains of Orcania. The People of the Mountains' squinty eyes and olive complexion are due to the harsh conditions of the mountains. They are a very superstitious and wary bunch because of the many illusions they face on mountains. The mountain spirits like to trick and endanger travelers so the people of the mountains always keep an eye out.

People of the Plains: A tribe that lives on the plains of Orcania. The People of the Plains blend in perfectly with their surroundings, which is one reason they are considered expert hunters. The plains people are a rather shy bunch and would rather avoid speaking with strangers.

People of the Water: A tribe that lives near the oceans of Orcania. The People of the Water spend most of their lives on boats and are expert fishermen. The strange designs on their bodies are actually birthmarks. Similar to a zebra's stripes, no two are ever the same. It is believed that this is their connection with the water spirit, Aquaritus.

Plague: Spirit of Sickness. Because of his name, most people believe that Plague is the cause of sicknesses in Orcania. This is, however, completely untrue. Plague prevents illnesses and is one of the main reasons why there are vaccines to some of Orcania's deadliest viruses.

Plue: Spirit of Happiness. Plue was born from the laughter of children and has thus retained a child-like outlook on life. He is considered one of the most sacred spirits in Orcania simply because Orcanians associate happiness with life. His trademark is the nonsense songs he sings. His singing causes happiness.

Quarpos: Currency used in Orcania, referred to as quarpos because the money can only be divided by four.

Racars: A creature indigenous to the null void zone. They are vicious hunters who will eat anything that moves. Their speed, endurance, and strength are not something to be trifled with.

Rainshay: A deadly high-class fiend. Rainshay are known for having the mad gene, which makes them perfect killing machines. The original rainshay was created from an assortment of animals. Because rainshay is composed of different animal parts, it is said that the creature went insane and killed everything in sight. It was finally slain by the great warrior Azul. Unfortunately, there are still people who try to create them today.

Sand Shark: A creature found within the deserts of Orcania. The sand shark moves through the sand similar to how its cousin moves through the water. They are known for preying on small animals and their dislike for the taste of human. Because of its poor eyesight, there have been a few sand shark attacks. Attacks can be avoided so long as one stays on a kadir.

Sapphire Rose: A legendary rose that is said to exist in Orcania. The Sapphire Rose is considered the balance between life and death because its petals can bring someone to life while its thorn can take life away. No one is quite sure where it is hidden.

Sea Horse: A creature created to carry man over water and earth. There are few sea horses left in the wild because the people of Orcania have domesticated them. They are actually faster on land than their cousins. The only downside is that they dehydrate easily.

Searchers: Servants to Shal Ron Lee who travel Orcania in search of new knowledge. Searchers usually take the form of owls but have also been seen as coyotes. Because of Shal Ron Lee's imprisonment, they are the only way he can receive new knowledge.

Seven Falls: Waterfalls that are considered sacred since there are so many falls so close together. Also, its last fall, the seventh, has baffled scholars for ages. No one is quite sure why the seventh waterfall travels upwards. Some believe it has to do with Shal Ron Lee's library.

Shal Ron Lee: Spirit of Knowledge. Shal Ron Lee has a devious nature and is greedy. Because of his mischievousness and his attempt to eat Gardenia, he was imprisoned within his library. If one wants to receive knowledge from Shal Ron Lee, then one has to be careful around Shal Ron Lee simply because he likes to outwit his opponents.

Shamballa Mountains: A mountain range situated in the western part of Orcania. The Shamballa Mountains are known for their many tall peaks. Many expert mountain climbers try to scale them but only a few have succeeded. Supposedly, the Council of Ten meeting grounds are within this mountain range.

Shinobi Tribe: A group of people who live at the base of the Shamballa Mountain range. The Shinobi wear animal masks over the upper half of their faces so that no one can see their identities. They believe that if someone were to see what they looked like then they would have power over them. The Shinobis are expert hunters who use their blowpipes in all sorts of ways. They dislike trespassers and will generally kill them on sight.

Sniper Plant: A carnivorous plant that uses poisonous darts to immobilize its prey. The sniper plant looks similar to its cousin, the ivy vine, except it has shinier leaves and bulbs with teeth. The leaves are used to attract its prey's attention. They have been known to eat animals as big as deer.

Srilo Village: A village on the border between the earth and desert regions. Srilo Village originally started out as a trading post but gradually grew into a small town. Even today, its main source of business is its trading post.

Terra: Spirit of Earth. Terra is laid back and has a peaceful outlook on life. She works with Gardenia but tends to get annoyed with Gardenia's paranoid behavior. They have clashed a few times, but they finally settled their differences when the Council of Ten threatened to confine them to their elements.

The Three Graces: A famous statue found within Crangor City. No one is sure of its origin because the Three Graces has been there since Crangor City was created. Each statue represents a grace that Orcania believes its citizens should possess.

Three Moons Grasslands: Grasslands named as such because it offers a perfect view of the three moons. Many babosas live there. It is said that a legendary health spring exists within the grasslands, but no one has been able to find it.

Toracs: A group of rebels who are opposed to the High Council's new laws. The Toracs are mainly composed of the different tribes. They hate the new laws simply because it threatens their way of life.

Travel Bus: The fastest form of transportation in Orcania. The travel bus only runs through the earth region and tends to have problems with dust storms following it. Engineers are still trying to figure out a way to stop this from occurring since people have had damage to their retinas from the dust flung into their eyes.

Twilight Falcon: A legendary creature in Quarteze. The Twilight Falcon was one of the original warriors to seal the Shadow One in the molten ball in the center of Quarteze. It is said that when he flies at night, stars become entangled within his tail feathers.

Underground City: The Underground City wasn't always underground. It was supposed to be an experimental community where new technologies could be used to decide if they could benefit the world. Unfortunately, the foundations were built on unstable ground, thus sending the city underground. Luckily, they were able to find a cave to the outside world. They tried to live underground; but due to the lack of light, many of the citizens went crazy so the city was abandoned.

Vent: A small seal-like creature that is able to produce huge gusts of wind. They originally came from the mountains. Vents are considered sacred to Aktoe, the Spirit of Wind, because of their abilities. Their bodies act like a balloon allowing them to absorb a huge volume of air. It is said that in ancient times, vents used this ability to float in the air. It allowed them to be able to get from one mountain to the next. Unfortunately, the modern-day vents do not seem to have this knowledge.

Whispering Fields: Fields found in Quarteze. The Whispering Fields received their name because on quiet nights, it sounds as if someone is whispering. Scholars have found it rather strange that this phenomenon only occurs when the weather is calm. The assumption is that the whispering occurs on windy days. In fact, one resident from a nearby village claims that on windy days, instead of whispering, the fields sound as if they are screaming.